THE UNKNOWN
CREATURES
AND THE TALKING
SPARROW

BY

IVAN GOLDING

Grosvenor House
Publishing Limited

The right of Ivan Golding to be identified as the author of this
work has been asserted in accordance with Section 78
of the Copyright, Designs and Patents Act 1988

The book cover picture is copyright to Ivan Golding

This book is published by
Grosvenor House Publishing Ltd
28-30 High Street, Guildford, Surrey, GU1 3EL.
www.grosvenorhousepublishing.co.uk

Please note that all the characters in this story are fictional.
And have no relation to anyone bearing the same name in the real world.

A CIP record for this book
is available from the British Library

ISBN 978-1-78623-016-4

CONTENTS

ACKNOWLEDGMENTS

First of all I would like to acknowledge and give thanks to our dear Lord Jesus Christ for giving me all these very special intimate Revelations. Many thanks to the editor who spent their time proof reading and corrected this book to make it enjoyable to the readers. My special thanks also go to my son Ivor and son-in-law Craig Morton and the rest of my family who have assisted in this project.

FOREWORD

Jeremy Ashman and David Whoot, the detective Doctor, are extraordinary people with special abilities. They are able to foretell of things to come and converse with creatures other than human beings. They use their special abilities to tell of forthcoming dangers.

JEREMY ASHMAN SAW A CREATURE
ON A TWIN MOONISLAND THAT LOOKED LIKE THIS

CHAPTER 1

ATTITUDE

Jeremy Ashman was lost for words when he looked through the window of his house and saw two young men; McCredie Dalton and his friend Morris Winters staggering up the road with bottles of drink in their hands. This was three weeks after they had failed their final exam and did not receive a place at the University.

McCredie and his friend Morris Winters were no strangers to Jeremy Ashman. They were born and raised by their parents in the same street as Jeremy.

The two students had spent many years studying at school and college and the time came for their final exam results. Some made the grade to attend University and some did not.

A few months after the two students overcame their sorrow of not going to University they came and visited Jeremy Ashman with a deep sadness filling their eyes.

'Hi, Jeremy,' McCredie said, 'we've come to let you know we've stop studying and our futures are ruined.'

Jeremy looked at them and saw how disappointed they were.

'Oh, I see,' said Jeremy, 'you've failed your exams but your futures don't have to be ruined. There are many people who didn't goes to University but had a successful life. So do not just throw the towel in!'

'Can I ask you a question,' Jeremy asks McCredie?

'Go ahead,' he replied with his head hung toward the ground.

'Let's just say for instance that you were walking home from college one day, you suddenly slipped and fell and weren't able to get up on your own, would you ask someone to give you a helping hand or would you just lay there for the rest of your life?'

As soon as Jeremy said this Morris looked at him saying, 'what are you getting at?'

'Your attitude can make a difference, help attain your goal or give up on it. It can even bring out the best in you or the worst. You've failed your exams but keep your chin up; you can try, try and try again, the ball is now in your Court,' he paused.

A few days had passed and Jeremy was surprised to see the two students once again bright and early, but this time he saw Morris Winters and his friend McCredie on their way to the library to borrow some books. As soon as they got to the door it started to rain.

McCredie looked at his friend saying, 'Morris see it is raining, we'll just look around until the rain stops.'

'Ok,' agreed Morris and they went to the shelves and took out some books and sat down for a quiet read. As soon as

McCredie opened one of the books he saw Jeremy Ashman's photograph in it.

'Wait a minute,' he uttered in astonishment, 'this book belongs to Jeremy Ashman!'

Morris looked sharply at him saying, 'Some people used to call him their guardian angel because he is a kind loving person.'

Nothing else was said as they sat down to study their books.

Years before Jeremy was known as a 'people protector' who often experienced times when he felt confused by the voices he heard in his head, which he couldn't explain.

One special day the most extraordinary thing happened. Quite by accident he met a Detective called Dr David Whoot who was head of a large private detective agency.

This was at a time when the agency required people of special abilities to join the organisation and the Detective thought Jeremy Ashman could be just the person he was looking for.

Shortly after eleven o'clock on the day after their meeting Jeremy had a surprise telephone call from Dr Whoot who asked him to come and see him at his office for a job interview. Jeremy couldn't believe his ears; Jeremy was filled with a mixture of anxiety and excitement at the prospect of being interviewed for a job.

The following morning as darkness gave way to the day, a nervous Jeremy jumped out of bed and dressed in preparation for his appointment, he was stood outside the Detective's office hours before it opened.

As Dr Whoot arrived at his office and greeted his colleagues he knelt down and started to pray, asking for God's help in making the right decisions.

After praying he immediately asked Jeremy if he would like to join the group and work with the underground force of detectives.

'Err yes,' uttered Jeremy, who was staggered in amazement at what just took place, as he was expecting a long drawn out interview, bearing in mind he was standing in such a prestigious organisation.

A few months had passed since joining the Detective's establishment when Jeremy was asked to take on a cold case assignment concerning a missing 13-year-old school girl who was presumed to have been abducted from her parents' home in 1977.

After Jeremy read his assignment he looked directly at Dr Whoot.

'Sir,' he uttered, 'we're now in the nineties. That crime was committed over 13 years ago.'

'Yes,' Dr Whoot agreed. 'Sergeant Ross believes there's a small possibility that the kidnapped girl might still be alive as her body had yet to be discovered.'

Then on one extraordinary night in June 1990, time appeared to move as quickly as a flash. 'Boom' Jeremy and his family just vanished into the unknown. Led by his spiritual abilities, they were taken on a journey, travelling back in time to late December 1977.

CHAPTER 2

THE CRUEL FOUR

As Jeremy reappeared, to his amazement he was stood outside the gate mid conversation with a stranger who was brushing the autumn leaves from the forecourt of his gate.

His wife Sally shouted to him. 'Jeremy dear, I'm going to the supermarket with the children. Would you like to come along with us?'

'Ok,' he said, 'why not?'

'We'll finish this chat later when I return,' he said to the stranger.

At this time most people had already done their Christmas shopping early to avoid the Christmas Eve crowds.

Without any further hesitation Jeremy, his wife and children went off to the supermarket, which wasn't far from where the Ashman's were living at the time.

The morning was very cold and the air was thin. While they were at the supermarket an old age pensioner came to shop next to them rubbing his hands together to keep them warm.

'Isn't it chilly today?' mumbled the old fellow, trying to start a chat with the Ashman's.

'Of course,' Jeremy answered, 'it is very chilly indeed.'

From one word to another Jeremy befriended the elderly gentleman. He gave his name as Joe Harris and explained that he lived alone and had no visitors over the Christmas period.

Mrs Ashman sympathised with the old man and before they parted company they made a promise to Joe that one of them would pay him a visit during the Christmas holidays. Joe Harris was very glad to hear this, they shook hands and said goodbye.

The days passed very quickly, it was now three days after Christmas. The Ashman's extended family, who came to spend the festive season with them, had returned to their own homes to celebrate the New Year.

Mrs Ashman was alone in the kitchen happily singing along to the radio.

Then a knock came at the door. Mrs Ashman shouted out from the dining room, 'Will someone please answer to the door?'

'Ok, mum,' replied Robert, her eldest son, who hurriedly went to the door. It was Richard – one of his young friends from the next street who had come to play with him. As Robert popped his head through the doorway he instantly shouted, 'Wow! Isn't it cold out here?'

'Yes,' Richard said, and it's misty but we can always play around here at your gate.'

The Ashman's home was not far from the avenue, just a few steps away from the road. Robert took a closer look around. 'Wait a minute,' he said to Richard, 'I'll ask mum if it's alright for us to play out here.'

He stood at the door and shouted, 'Mum, can me and Richard play outside our gate?'

Before Mrs, Ashman replied she took a look through the kitchen window and saw how misty it was. She knew quite well that it could be dangerous for children to play at the side of the road in the mist. She shouted, 'No, Robert, it's too misty out there, but if you and Richard want to come inside and play with your toys you got for Christmas you can.'

'Ok, mum,' he uttered gladly. Then his mother shouted again, 'Before you come in to play, tell him that he should go home and let his parents know where he is.'

As soon as Richard heard this, he ran home to let his mother know that he was going to be playing at his friend's house. Robert waited for him at the door until he returned and they went inside to play in the living room. Jeremy, Robert's father, was already in his favourite chair keeping an eye on Alvin, their youngest son. He was playing with the toys he had received for Christmas.

As soon as the boys entered into the living room Richard said, 'Hi, Mr Ashman.'

'Hi, Richard, how was your Christmas?' Jeremy replied.

'It was ok,' he smiled.

'Well,' said Jeremy, 'now that you're here, Robert, you and your friend can play with your younger brother.'

'Ok, Dad,' he agreed. He and his friend went to a corner of the room to play with their toys whilst his younger brother Alvin played with his pull back to run cars.

While Jeremy was sat looking on affectionately at the children playing with their toys his wife Sally suddenly entered the room filled with the spirit of Christmas! She twirled around the room, laughing.

Then she stopped and gave her husband a kiss on the chin and whispered close to his ears. 'My darling, you might not have remembered this, but we made a promise to pay old Harris a visit at Christmas. Now it's three days after Christmas, poor old Harris!'

Jeremy breathed out with a sigh as he realised that since the day they met Joe Harris at the supermarket time had passed so quickly. He couldn't believe that it was the 28th of December already.

No sooner had Sally left the room; she took two steps backwards and turned around. She went through the living room door into the small passageway, 'Children!' she shouted, 'go and wash your hands.'

Lunch was about to be served, so the children washed their hands and took their seats at the table.

West Indian food was part of the menu! It was great fun for Jeremy to teach his English born children to eat West Indian food! The sweet potatoes were good but the yam they weren't too sure of. But there was roast beef, fried chicken, Brussels sprouts, Yorkshire pudding, gravy, roast potatoes and lots of other goodies on the table. Everybody had an excellent and enjoyable meal.

Had Sally known that after lunch her husband would be going to visit Mr Harris she might not have reminded him until the next day. She had wanted to visit Mr Harris with her husband but didn't want to disturb the playing children.

However, after they had eaten Jeremy got dressed and ready to visit Mr Harris; he didn't want to disappoint the old fellow, especially as it was Christmas.

Just as he was about to go through the door, he shouted to his wife, 'Sally, I'm going now, as nobody else is going with me!'

Sally came and walked with him to the door and gave him a goodbye kiss, but was sad to see him go without her.

As Jeremy was on his way to Mr Harris's place he began thinking about the Biblical words that his wife had rehearsed at Christmas. It was about Jesus's birthday, from the Holy Bible, Saint Luke Chapter 2 verse 14 which said, 'Glory to God in the highest, and on earth, peace, and good will towards men'; of course meaning women and children as well.

As the day wore on Jeremy found himself in the neighbourhood not far from the rural community in which old Harris lived.

He walked to the outskirts of the village and stopped for a moment to look around the area, although he couldn't see very far as the day was still cold and misty. It was the winter months and the cold mist lingered, making it seem later than it actually was.

Mr Harris was the owner of a large semi-detached house in the rural community and when Jeremy arrived he had a shock. The house had been recently modernised and looked brand new compared to the others. An old sign hung on the gate: 'Beware of the dogs.' Jeremy could have ignored the sign, as

Harris hadn't mentioned owning any dogs, but chose to stand outside, unsure if the old man still lived there.

He took a long look up and down the lane and suspected that he'd come to the wrong address, but he acted bravely and went through the gate to the door of the house.

As he was about to ring the doorbell he heard someone digging. He stood at the door and continued to listen. The digging sound was coming from the backyard.

'Wait a minute,' he said to himself. He knew that Mr Harris was old and fragile so it couldn't be him that was digging. If it wasn't Mr Harris digging then who could it be? It was understandable for Jeremy to be apprehensive in this situation as it was the Christmas period and only certain people would be out digging during these times. It could have been the gas people or Mr Harris could have a burst water pipe. Could the Water Board be there to fix it? Then he had further thoughts; if it was the Water Board where were their vehicles parked? There weren't any such vehicles parked in the lane.

With all these thoughts he left the doorway and tiptoed towards the backyard for a closer look. All this suspicious activity had brought to light a crime that had been committed at that very place three days after Christmas in 1977. Was Jeremy there to find out how the crime happened and who was responsible? He sneaked a little nearer to see that was digging, whilst being careful not to make the person aware that he was there.

As soon as he got close enough to see he caught sight of a man digging a hole that looked like a shallow grave, Jeremy began to panic. The man was of a dark complexion; he had a well-built body and a very mean looking face, he was wearing a white vest and dark trousers. The man was hard at work.

His face was sweaty and his body steaming, as if he had caught fire on this cold winter's day.

'Good gracious,' Jeremy uttered in a frightened tone of voice. He thought the man might have murdered Mr Harris and was now digging a shallow grave to bury him in.

As soon as he thought about it he felt this strange feeling come over him, his legs weakened in fear. He looked again and saw something hanging from the handle of his shovel. It was a glove a black leather glove to be precise; the other was lying on the ground beside him.

It was clear that something odd was going on, but as scared as he was Jeremy decided to keep his cool and wait. Hopefully, he might witness who was to be buried in the shallow grave. He didn't have to wait long as the man suddenly stopped digging and left his pickaxe lying on the frozen ground beside the hole he had made.

Jeremy stood still, looking on in dread at what was to follow. The man didn't know that somebody was watching him. He returned to the shallow grave carrying a large roll of plastic material that he could barely manage. Finally, he dragged it up close to the hole.

This was very alarming but Jeremy knew quite well that if he wanted to see what the guy was going to do with the roll of plastic material he would have to keep himself composed.

After he put the roll of plastic material close to the hole he went away and fetched a young white female's body to the shallow grave. He laid her lifeless body on the ice-cold ground.

When Jeremy saw this he hastily covered his mouth and shuddered at the sight of the dead girl's lifeless body. Then he reminded himself of what Detective Ross had once told him. If he saw someone committing a crime in the field of his vision, the victim might not necessarily have died in real life; this may only be to reveal what was about to happen.

Jeremy was terrified but kept on telling himself not to be alarmed as he glared terrifyingly at the young girl's frozen body. Had she just been killed or had she been left outside all night in the cold.

Her long dark hair had spread out across the ground and over her shoulders. Her dress was made of a black and white spotted material. Suddenly Jeremy thought; 'I wonder if she had been kidnapped and taken to Mr Harris's home to be buried in his backyard?' he said to himself.

Despite being a witness to murder, Jeremy tried to hold his nerve and not panic. What he didn't know at the time was the worst was yet to come. He still hadn't seen Joe Harris and a dead girl's body was lying on the ground, waiting to be buried. He began wondering if old Harris was a victim. Is he already dead and buried somewhere in a shallow grave in his own backyard?

He then realised he was standing too close to the horrifying scene. He dare not move, as the gravedigger was likely to see him. He thought of crying out for help but the neighbouring houses were in complete darkness.

The suspect would know that Jeremy had seen the dead girl, him digging the shallow grave and wouldn't allow him to escape. In his mind he thought that bad people are always the most aggressive people and if seen by the gravedigger, he would be dealt with without mercy.

Poor Jeremy, he was scared half to death and now realised he could be harmed. Whilst the gravedigger was busy he tried to sneak away but the man spotted him moving. He was startled but not for long and soon regained his composure and shouted out in a nervy tone of voice, 'We've got a visitor!'

Jeremy didn't see anybody else at the time and wondered who this man was shouting to. He soon got a massive surprise as he saw three other men running out of Mr Harris's house to stand with the gravedigger at the edge of the shallow grave.

The four people stared at Jeremy then glanced at the dead girl's body lying on the ground. They looked at each other without saying a word. It seemed as though they could understand each other's thoughts.

Now Jeremy was face-to-face with four men who were probably responsible for the death of the young girl.

Jeremy knew very well that he was a witness to a crime. He couldn't hang around any longer or he would be the next to be murdered.

He began thinking that if they wanted to kill him they would have to catch him first and that wasn't going to be easy. He noticed the four men whispering to each other. He listened intently trying to make out what they were saying. He expected that they might be planning to trap him and accuse him of being the killer. He weighed up the situation and knew that he hadn't much time to escape and couldn't hesitate any longer. The gravedigger was the only black person in the bunch of men. He was very tall with a muscular physique and was like a giant in comparison to Jeremy.

Jeremy believed that one of the three men that came out of Mr Harris's house might be the boss. He was of medium build and average height, clean-shaven and very smartly dressed. He looked at Jeremy with a devilish glint in his eyes, 'How can we help you?' he asked in a deep, crusty tone of voice.

He guessed that they had planned to keep him on the premises, so he decided to make a quick exit through the garden. Then to his error, he completely miscalculated the condition of the garden expecting the ground to be completely frozen solid. In fact parts of it had been recently ploughed up and there were large muddy patches, which were extremely sloppy. The four men began to advance and positioned themselves between him and the edge of the garden. Jeremy immediately took a running leap but to his dismay he landed ankle deep in the soft, muddy clay. He struggled and grabbed hold of a broken wooden fence and pulled himself out of the mud.

He hurried and clambered up the fencing, bundling himself over the top with all his might, landing back in the lane. As soon as he fell he saw one of the guys give chase. Jeremy wondered why the other three men didn't also chase him, was he just the youngest of the four? He didn't know this, but just after he had gone the three men that stayed behind hid the dead girl's body elsewhere and covered up the shallow grave. Jeremy ran and ran until he came to a road junction. He followed the road signs that lead towards the city centre. Hopefully on the way he might come across a police officer or seek someone's help. He must have run for about two miles and slowed down to catch his breath. He looked and saw the guy chasing him had almost caught up. So he started running again and as the chase progressed towards the city the guy shouted, 'We are the Cruel Four!'

'Yes,' Jeremy replied, 'I should have known that because humans would have a better name.'

The man shouted out again, 'You know why we can't let you escape? You've now heard our secret code name.'

Jeremy had never heard of the Cruel Four and certainly never come across any secret code name. The only thing he did know was that he had seen a man digging a shallow grave, a girl's dead body lying on the ground waiting to be buried and another three men exiting Mr Harris's house. On top of this Jeremy had not yet established what had happened to old Joe Harris.

In the midst of despair Jeremy hadn't noticed that he must have slowed down and the guy chasing him had gained ground until he suddenly felt someone grab hold of his shirt from behind saying, 'I've caught you!' The man shoved him in the back saying, 'Walk on in front of me.'

A panic-stricken Jeremy dare not argue as he'd already seen what they were capable of.

As the two were on their way back, the man took Jeremy through a narrow series of backstreets where he had a small closed-up van parked, waiting. He forced Jeremy to drive him to his hide out, which was among an outcrop of stones.

As soon as they got there a middle aged, dark-skinned woman came to the door. She looked at Jeremy from head to toe. Then she looked at the man and said, 'I see, you've fetched me a live one this time instead of your usual blood-stained clothes for me to wash.'

As soon as she said this, the guy pushed her out of the way saying, 'I am leaving him here with you for a while, but I'll be back before you can blink an eye.'

CHAPTER 3

THE DREADED STUFF

She looked sharply at him and said, 'Did I hear you say that you're leaving him here with me?'

'Yes,' he gasped, 'what's wrong with that? I'll tie him up before I go. If he attempts to break loose just give him some of the stuff.' He pointed to the white, thick liquid in a jar.

Then he tied Jeremy's hands and feet saying, 'I'm going now, but I'll be back soon with my friends. Please don't let him go.' He got into his van and drove away.

Now that the kidnapper had gone and the woman was alone Jeremy began to think about how he'd approach her in a calm and peaceful way so as not to alarm her.

'Madam,' he said.

The woman turned her eyes and looked at him but didn't reply.

She went and picked up the jar with the deadly stuff and fetched a spoon with it. She came to Jeremy with a spoon full of the stuff. 'Open your mouth,' she said, 'drinks this.'

'No,' Jeremy said, 'I will not drink it. Tell me what it is.'

'Ok,' she spoke angrily. She went and fetched a rusty box of assorted weapons saying, 'If you do not drink the stuff when he returns he will kill you with one of these.' She pointed at the box.

Jeremy glared at the rusty box of weapons but there wasn't a gun in it.

When Jeremy had regained his sanity he uttered, 'Woman, before you kill me, I think you should know that the police are looking for me. Someone saw your man-friend kidnap me in his closed-up van and is heading this way.'

She looked at him but didn't reply. He spoke again, 'You might not know this yet, but your friends have kidnapped and murdered an innocent young girl. I have discovered that today and written it down. It was three days after Christmas 1977. I was an eyewitness to the crime. Since then they have tried to kill me, so nobody is left as a witness to their cruelty. They also accused me of overhearing a secret code word that they use whenever anyone is to be kidnapped by them.

'I think it's strange that they have also accused me of hearing their secret name, "The Cruel Four". They said that nobody else knows them by this name, not even the police, at least not yet. Woman, you may or may not know this, but your man-friend and his three colleagues have also been responsible for the abduction of many other young girls in and around the area; many of the bodies have not yet been discovered.

As soon as he said this, the woman just casually lifted her shoulder as to say, 'so what?' Yet the fact still remained that in spite of trying to force feed Jeremy with the dreaded 'stuff' he still had a feeling the woman didn't intend to kill him but just to terrify him.

Jeremy knew quite well that time wasn't on his side as the woman's boyfriend could return at any time. Worst of all he'd bring his three colleagues with him to see that Jeremy had a slow and painful death. The woman must have known this as she had a change of mind. She went outside and had a good, long look around the area. She returned quickly and cut the string from Jeremy's hands and feet.

'You can go now,' she said, 'you better hurry up before he returns.'

As soon as she said this, Jeremy left the place like a wild bird escaping from its cage. He couldn't believe that she had set him free. As soon as he able to, he ran and ran, as fast as he could.

He struggled over the stony hillside until he came to the main road. To his horror he realised that the Pennine Way had two-way traffic, one way to Manchester the other way towards Huddersfield and Leeds. God only knows which way the kidnapper might approach from, but by this time it was getting closer to evening.

With watchful eyes, Jeremy made his way nervously and stood at the bus stop. Hopefully the bus from Manchester to Leeds might come along before the kidnapper returned. He waited at the bus stop in fear, looking here and there for about ten minutes and then to his relief the bus came.

So far so good, he breathed out with a sigh of relief and made his way upstairs and sat at the back of the bus. He was exhausted. He must have quickly dozed off until he felt someone shaking him saying, 'Wake up, dozy, dozy, wake up!'

He woke up with a leap and got off the bus and from the station it was just a short distance to home. Soon he found himself around the corner from his house. When he got there he began knocking at the door because he had forgotten to take his key with him.

His wife came quickly and let him in.

'Darling!' she cried glad to see him. She tried to give him a welcome home kiss but to her surprise kissing his lifeless lips alarmed her. 'Oh my God,' she uttered, frightened, 'what has happened to you? Are you ill?'

Jeremy was tired and short of breath so didn't immediately reply to his wife's question. He just walked inside with her and as they were going through the small passageway towards the living room his legs buckled beneath him. She thought he was suffering from some cold-related illness, as he didn't have any bruises on his body that she could see.

She helped him into the living room and sat him down in his favoured armchair where he leaned back to rest.

'Thank you very much,' he said.

He decided to rest there for a while but his wife disagreed saying, 'Oh, no I'm going to call for your doctor'. She telephoned but as it was out of the surgery's hours she left a message asking for the doctor to visit the next morning.

After the doctor had visited, Jeremy began to explain the situation to his wife as best he could. When she heard, she looked at him and breathed out with a sigh of relief and sat down, worried that her husband was in some kind of trouble.

Jeremy saw her looking worried and said softly, 'My darling, please do not worry – we'll be ok!'

'Oh, no,' she spoke through her tears. 'Let's go to the police. You can tell them what the Cruel Four have done to you and ask for police protection.'

'No,' Jeremy said, 'we can go to the police, but not yet.'

'Why?' She asked in an upset tone of voice. Instead of replying he went and sat close to her and put his hands around her saying, 'I have told you, dear, that I had a mission to perform. I have to trace a missing schoolgirl who disappeared in 1977 and report my findings to Detective Doctor Whoot. Jeremy knew that the police wouldn't be able to keep an eye on the family everywhere they went.

By this time, New Year's Day 1978 had passed.

The next day Jeremy asked Whoot to send some of his men to the murder scene and next morning the police arrived. One officer asked Jeremy to make a statement of all that he knew about the Cruel Four gang.

As soon as Detective Mullins read the statement he asked Jeremy and his wife to accompany them to the place where he had seen the Cruel Four bury the girl in the shallow grave.

From where the Ashman's lived it was only a short drive to the neighbourhood.

As soon as the officers arrived at old Harris' home some of them went to search the house and some went to the shallow grave in the backyard. By this time, of course, the grave was level with the ground and the gang had long gone.

Detective Whoot has sent some of his expert officers to work with Detective Mullins to see if they could recover the dead girl's body.

Three officers who examined the ground acknowledged that the earth had been disturbed recently and marked the spot where the shallow grave was. Detective Mullins called some of his officers and asked them to fetch shovels, saying, 'Come on lads, let's dig her up.'

The officers began by carefully shovelling the dirt until they came upon some thick plastic materials that the Cruel Four had used to cover up the girl's body in the grave. They carefully removed the covering and were surprised to find that the girl's body wasn't there.

The Cruel Four had covered up the empty shallow grave to confuse the police as to where the dead girl may be resting. One of officers looked at the other and said, 'Have you ever seen anything like this?'

'Oh no,' he said, 'never.' They were absolutely stunned at the scene. Detective Mullins went and looked at the shallow grave.

'Jeremy,' he shouted, 'can you give us some more details about the dead girl's body that you saw lying here three days after Christmas 1977? Did you actually see the Cruel Four bury the dead girl's body in this shallow grave?'

'No, sir,' Jeremy said, 'I saw the man who was digging the grave fetch a roll of plastic sheeting. He fetched the dead girl's body and laid her out beside the grave.'

Then he described the four men to the officers saying that one of them had given chase, so he didn't know if the others had buried the girl or taken her body away with them.

While they were debating the matter one of the officers received a telephone call. Someone had given them a tip-off that a member of the gang used to live at the side of the road that led towards the city.

Some of the officers thought the killers might have taken the dead girl's body in the boot of their car and dumped her somewhere else. While they were debating the situation Jeremy and his wife went to see a friend who lived not far from where they were. As they were on the way walking to their friend's home they saw a member of the Church who told them that a prayer meeting was being held at the church where their friend was the minister, so they took a detour and went there instead.

As soon as they went into the church they heard that the pastor they knew was moving her ministry elsewhere, but as soon as the pastor saw Jeremy and his wife she went to greet them with outstretched arms. She might have heard about the great temptation that they had suffered at the hands of the Cruel Four gang. The pastor took them with her to the altar to pray and rested one of her hands on each of their shoulders. After she had prayed they got up again and the pastor told them that she was moving her ministry to another church and a new minister was to replace her. As soon as the pastor heard that the new minister had arrived in the church she went to make him feel welcome before she left. Jeremy left his wife upstairs talking with friends and went downstairs with the pastor.

As soon as they entered the church hall, he looked and saw some of the members sitting beside a fire, which was starting to die out.

'Pastor,' he said, 'I'm saying goodbye to you now because I don't know if you'll still be here when I return. I'm going to the woodland across the road to gather some pieces of wood as the fire at the church is dying out.'

Jeremy walked towards the woodland across the road. There was also a short cut through the woodland that led to a main road and at the bottom of the field was a Y-junction.

CHAPTER 4

THE GANG OF YOUTHS

As Jeremy was walking towards the woodland he bumped into a cousin.

'Dudley!' he shouted out joyfully, he was glad to see him.
So he stopped and waited until Dudley caught him up they greeted each other with a friendly hug.

Dudley looked at him saying, 'Are you going to the woodland?'

'Yes,' he replied 'I'm going there to get some pieces of wood for the fire at the church, as it is dying out. Are you coming with me?'

'Oh, no, my brother,' he replied in a fearful tone of voice.

'Why?' Jeremy asked. Instead of replying, Dudley turned his eyes and looked towards the woodland.

Jeremy wasn't aware that some time ago a dead girl's body had been found there. Then Dudley told him that a body had been discovered there and ever since he'd chosen not to go there.

As soon as he said this, Jeremy began thinking that it could be the body of the dead girl, which the Cruel Four gang had taken from the shallow grave in Mr Harris's backyard.

Having all these thoughts he looked sharply at his cousin, 'Dudley,' he declared, 'can you please tell me more about the dead girl's body that was found on this woodland? How long ago was it?'

Dudley went silent for a minute and looked at Jeremy.

'Why are you asking me all these questions? Am I a suspect to the crime?'

'Oh, no, good gracious,' Jeremy said, 'there is a very good reason why I'm asking. More than less we shouldn't be afraid of the dead, as those who are dead are dead. We should be more careful of those who are alive.'

While they were talking someone threw a stone from the hillside nearby. The stone landed in the main road and bounced once or twice before it came to rest on Jeremy's shoes. Dudley saw how close it was from hitting them.

'Wow!' He cried out and looked up to the hill. They knew quite well that this could have been a tragic accident as the stone could have hit passing traffic.

Dudley regained his self-control and took a look around the hillside and angrily shouted. 'Whoever it was that threw a stone down here, I dare you to come out and show yourself to us.'

As soon as he spoke a group of angry youths came running down the hill towards them. Jeremy and Dudley looked and saw they were outnumbered by the youths so they began to run. They took a short cut that led through the woodland and headed toward the Y-junction at the bottom of the field. Dudley was so afraid of the gang he had totally forgotten about being afraid of going through the woodland. As they fled, the youths must have taken a short cut and got to the Y-junction before them.

From there they began shouting, 'this road is the only way back to where you came from. The only way you'll get back there is if you give us your money, then no harm will come to you.' All this was a revelation of the days and the times of lawless generations to come.

At the Y-junction the youths began laughing and making a noise.

Dudley heard them and cried out, 'Oh boy, oh boy,' he cried, 'Jeremy, I'm scared.'

Jeremy looked at him and could see his teeth were chattering and his legs were wobbly. Dudley said, 'let's gives them our money then they might not harm us.'

Jeremy looked sharply at him and said, 'I'm glad that you say, our money, if it is our money why should we give it to them?'

Before they got to the main road Jeremy stopped at the side of the path. Dudley stood looking at him. He took off one of his shoes and put the money he had into his sock. All the money he had that day was £4.06p.

By this time they had come to the main road, but the Y-junction was still a little distance away from where they were. They saw some people waiting for the bus and made their way to the bus stop and stood with them. The gang of youths saw them at the bus stop and decided to leave the Y-junction. When they came to the bus stop they bullied their way past the people waiting in the queue. Jeremy thought hopefully that the youths wouldn't start any trouble at the bus stop.

But he was wrong and one of them looked at Dudley and he began to panic. 'You can have my money,' he told them.

'Oh, no, Jeremy, said, 'you're not giving them any money.' He thought that they would do the same to the other passengers and while they stood there arguing the bus almost filled with passengers. The gang of youths didn't have the least regard for those who were first waiting in the queue. They pushed their way on to the bus before the others and took the empty seats. Those youths who didn't have a seat stood in the way chatting and prevented others getting onto the bus. One of them, who was the biggest bully, bumped into a lady passenger, 'Get your legs out of my way,' he said.

At this point, let it be known that this story might be telling of things that might already happen or of things to come. At this time the youths were behaving badly against their elders. This was a call to remember the days that we live in. Jeremy looked at his cousin Dudley. They were sure the little devils intended to hurt someone and to add to a bad situation, someone had left their garden tools on the bus seats at the back. There was a chopper and some other equipment. Perhaps they had forgot to take the garden equipment with them? While Jeremy was talking with one of the youths another took the chopper from the seat.

Jeremy said, 'Young man, please put the chopper down as you may cause an accident.' As soon as he said this, he acted bravely and took the weapon away from the youth.

After he had taken the chopper there came a voice from a person unseen saying, 'Jeremy Ashman, please tell the youths that they should learn to be kind towards one another!'

As soon as the youth heard the voice of the unseen person they immediately repented of their wrongdoings and returned all that they had stolen. After that they got off the bus, they ran all the way to the hillside from whence they had first come. As soon as the youths had gone, Dudley breathed out with a sigh of relief. Not long after the youths had gone Jeremy and his cousin got off the bus and parted company. As Jeremy was on his way back to the church a police car came up and stopped beside him. One of the officers came out of the car to ask him some questions.

Sally was waiting at the church and saw the policeman talking with her husband and she was scared stiff. She thought that he was in some kind of trouble with the law. She timidly went through the door to see what was happening.

As the Police Officer saw that she was worried he said, 'don't be alarmed, madam. Nothing is wrong. I'm just having a talk with your husband about a gang of troublesome youths on the bus not long ago.'

Sally dried the tears from her eyes and was glad everything was okay.

As soon as the police officers had gone another police car arrived with Detective Whoot's men, who had come to take them back home. As soon as they were in the car one of the officers said, 'Jeremy, we haven't a trace of the girl's body yet, nor where your friend old Harris has gone to. Don't worry; we won't leave a stone unturned until we find them.'

They couldn't understand why the Cruel Four had taken the dead girl's body with them and the same could have happened to old Harris. 'We'll extend our investigation until we find the Cruel Four and discover all their victims.' 'That's a promise,' said Detective Mullins, as they drove away.

CHAPTER 5

DEATH IN THE CITY

On 19 November 1978, Detective Allan had a tip that another young girl was about to be murdered by the Cruel Four but he didn't know when or where the crime might be committed. The hint came six months before the actual crime was to happen and he had no idea who was going to be killed.

One morning Sally woke up and was out of bed just in time to answer the telephone. The phone call came early while the children were in bed asleep.

It was an urgent call for her husband so she went immediately back up the stairs to give him the message.

'Darling,' she spoke as she went through the door, 'there was a telephone call for you from a Detective Sergeant Allan. Do you know who that is?'

'Yes,' he said, he's one of Dr Whoot's men.'

'I see,' she muttered, 'the Detective said can you please report to him at a house in the city?'

She gave him the address and the time of the appointment – 9.30 am. Although he didn't know what it was about he was out of bed quickly to get ready.

Then he took a look at the time. 'Good gracious!' He couldn't hesitate any longer as it was getting close to the time of the appointment.

From the Ashman's house it was only a short drive to the city. As he was about to leave Sally kissed him saying, 'Darling, be careful.'

As he went through the door he reminded her to keep a close watch on the children and see that they did not talk to strangers, unless they identified themselves to her. Neither should she allow the children to play out too far away from home.

After a short drive he found himself in the city. It was rush hour, so it took him a little time to cross over to the house to meet Detective Allan. When he got there he noticed that the police had marked off a spot of ground at the side of a building as if a crime has been committed there recently.

He wondered why Detective Allan would want to see him at a crime scene so early in the morning, but there was no answer to this ambiguous question.

As he was there with a mind full of thoughts a police officer came to escort him to the place where Allan was waiting. As soon as Jeremy and the officer went into the room the Detective got up from his seat, shook hands and gave his name.

Then he showed Jeremy to a seat and sat down. After a friendly chat Detective Allan took Jeremy and some officers to the place where the young deceased used to work.

After they had taken a look around they went to the mortuary to have a look at the deceased's body.

Jeremy was a bit nervy, as he'd never seen a dead person so close before. He shuddered at the very sight of the dead girl's body. He took a look at the face.

'Wait a minute,' he said. 'I can't be sure but I think I've seen this girl when she was alive'. He thought for a few minutes and it all came back to him. One day a few weeks ago while he was in the city and was about to cross the road a girl ran passed him saying, 'Please call the police for me, someone is trying to kill me.' Then she ran on without saying whereabouts.

'Young lady,' Jeremy had shouted out aloud, 'you haven't given your name. Where can the police find you?'

But by this time she was too far away to hear what Jeremy said.

As soon as he said this, they all looked at him. 'Do you think this is the same girl?' an officer asked.

Jeremy looked at the girl's face again and even though she looked just like her he couldn't be completely certain.

'How long ago was that?' another officer asked. 'Well, Jeremy declared, 'I think it was about two to three weeks ago.' The officer suggested that the young lady might have caught someone stealing and the person might have given her a quick blow and thrown her through the window of the house so that it might look like a case of suicide.

As soon as he said this, Detective Allan decided that they should go back to the house and examine the case more closely.

The officers went back to the house and started a new search of the room where the girl usually worked. Hopefully they might find the murder weapon. They searched the room for several hours looking for the weapon, but there was no trace of it. They went to one of the windows from which the killer could have thrown the girl to her death. Jeremy looked towards the ground; it was very scary, as he was afraid of heights.

As they were standing there debating the situation Detective Allan looked suddenly at Jeremy and said, 'I suggest that we will have to find the murder weapon or we haven't got a case.'

Jeremy and the other officers applied all their abilities and put their ideas into action and Allan was astonished at the detective work that enabled them to find the murder weapon.

The killer had hidden the weapon on the inner ledge of the wall in the room where the victim used to work. Detective Allan shook hands with Jeremy and his group of officers. He was delighted that the murder weapon had been discovered.

Allan took a long look at the weapon. 'Most incredible,' he said, seeing that the girl's bloodstains were on the knife. He clinched his fists with the weapon in it and said, 'Yes!' Now we've found the weapon it's time to solve the crime!'

Allan gave it to one of his officers saying, 'Put the weapon back, place it just where it was before.'

The officer took the weapon, climbed onto a desk and placed it back where they had found it. Then the Detective took a seat at the desk where he thought the deceased had sat when she had been attacked by the killer.

After he had replaced the weapon the Detective sat in silence for a minute, tapping his pen on the desk. Then he said,

'Jeremy, please open the door and go outside then shut it behind you. Wait there for a few minutes and, then come back inside'.

'Ok,' Jeremy agreed. He went outside and shut the door behind him then waited a moment or so and went in again. As soon as he came through the door Allan immediately got up out of his seat. 'Do you understand what I'm trying to prove, Jeremy?'

'Of course,' Jeremy replied without hesitation. 'I've got the picture. Whoever it was that killed the young lady it was an inside job.'

As soon as he said this they all clapped, 'Well done Jeremy!'

Some of them shook hands with him saying, 'Good work chap, good work; a job well done.'

Now the case had been solved, he marked the date in the middle of his hand – 16 March 1979.

Now that the crime had been solved Detective Allan said that he'd send local officers to make an arrest.

CHAPTER 6

THE COLD CASE ASSIGNMENT

Three weeks had passed since the officers had solved the crime of the young girl's murder.

One day when Jeremy was alone he decided to go and search for the for missing files for 1977 and as he was doing so he reminded himself of what Detective Mullins had once told him. He said that some of his guardians had special abilities and were able to work in all departments. That's why he gave Jeremy a job in the department – so that he might share his experience with the other officers.

After he had said this he shook hands with Jeremy saying, 'Good luck. Don't forget to report any progress you've made to Dr Whoot. See you soon.'

'Thank you sir,' he replied. Nothing else was said and they went on their way.

Two weeks later Jeremy went to bed and found himself retracing the last movements of the missing schoolgirl. It had come to light that one morning in July 1977 young Gillian Walters and her friend Jessica Wilmot trotted off happily to school.

The two girls came from well-to-do families – some people called them first class citizens. Despite this, their parents had brought them up in a deprived area, so they had many local friends. Gillian was just a few weeks older than Jessica.

The two girls had been best friends from a young age and were happy to live in a poor environment and to set an example to other children that a good education meant a brighter future.

As the years wore on, Gillian's mother, Cordelia, began having sleepless nights worrying about Gillian. She had turned 13 and started hanging out with girls much older than her and who were up to no good.

One day Jessica had a shocking experience when Gillian didn't want Jessica to be her friend any more. That day Jessica found out that bad company changes good peoples' lives.

The bright future that Gillian's parents had painted for their daughter to become a doctor was now growing dim. Cordelia could no longer sit at ease. She was afraid that the safety of her daughter had been threatened and there were rumours going round the neighbourhood that a serial killer was on the loose.

Young Gillian had been walking alone, taking a short cut though dark and creepy places to visit her friend's flat It wasn't until Gillian came home again that her mother breathed a sigh of relief that she was back home safely. Gillian was a very beautiful, 13-year-old schoolgirl. She sometimes wore make-up that made her more alluring to older men and she looked more like an adult than a schoolgirl.

One afternoon Gillian came home from school filled with excitement.

'Hi Mum,' she uttered as she came through the door. 'Is Dad home yet?' Instead of replying Mrs Walters turned and glared at her, 'Your Dad hasn't come home yet.'

'It's ok mum,' she said. Then she went running up the stairs to her bedroom, made a quick change of clothes and ran back downstairs.

'I'm going to see my friends and won't be back until the morning.'

'Excuse me!' Mrs Walters breathed out astonished. 'Gillian, you've just come home from school,' she paused.

'So what's wrong with that?' she asked with a crumpled look on her face and her lips began quivering, as she was ready to cry.

'Gillian, dear you're not allowed to stay out all night with your adult friend. You are going to school in the morning.'

As soon as she said this Gillian got upset, puffed at her mother and ran upstairs to her bedroom. She slung herself across her bed and started to sob as a spoiled child would. She thought hopefully that when her father came home he'd allow her to go and sleep at her friend's.

As soon as William came through the door she began sobbing again. Cordelia went quickly to meet him in the passageway. She kissed him and took his hand and explained that Gillian was behaving badly as she wasn't allowed to go and stay the night with her adult friend.

'So where's Gillian now?' he asked. Cordelia pointed her finger upstairs. 'She's locked herself in her room.'

Mr Walters went immediately upstairs and knocked at the bedroom door. 'Gillian, it's your dad, can I come in?'

'Yes,' she replied. The door was unlocked and after a long talk she dried the tears from her eyes.

As her father was going back down the stairs she spoke a parable, 'If I was in a chess set and I was the Queen. I would have taken up my position here and there and then it would be check mate!'

Mr Walters heard this and shook his head. He didn't know what on earth his daughter was talking about.

The next day Mrs Walters decided to go to the supermarket where she met one of her daughter's school friends, Isabella. As soon as she saw Mrs Walter she went to greet her, 'Hi, Mrs, Walters.'

'Hi, dear,' she replied. Then Isabella said softly, 'Where is Gillian today?'

'She's at school I hope!' she replied, looking at Isabella. When she saw a look of sadness on Isabella's face she knew that something was wrong.

Isabella told Mrs Walters that she'd seen a change in Gillian lately and she doesn't talk any more about her future career as a doctor. She usually told her friends how much she would love to be a doctor and her wish to help sick and disabled people get well again. Now it seemed that she had lost that vision completely.

Isabella could have told Mrs Walters many other things about her, but she had promised to keep this secret as friends. Mrs Walters would have panicked if she had known.

There is an old saying that things, which are hidden in the darkness, will eventually come to light.

On this particular day that saying did come to light. Gillian came home from school earlier than usual and unbeknown to her, mother had a trick up her sleeve.

Mrs Walters thought that her daughter had heeded good instructions and come home earlier than usual. But had she?

Mrs Walters didn't know this, but before Gillian came home from school her new adult friend had prompted her to go with her to an all-night social gathering. But the secret was this; she shouldn't let her parents know that she would be going out later that night. The question Gillian had asked her friend was, 'how can I leave home at night without letting my parents known where I'm going?'

'Well,' her friend had replied, 'all you have to do is pretend you're going to bed early and wait until your parents go to bed. Then you can get dressed and come to my flat.'

Gillian heeded her friend's bad advice and as soon as her parents went to bed and settled down to sleep she got dressed and tiptoed down the stairs.

As soon as she went through the door into the avenue she took off her shoes and started to run until she got to the top of the road. She stood for a minute to catch her breath, put on her shoes and set off walking.

To get to her friend's flat quickly Gillian took a shortcut that was dark and creepy. As soon as she came to the road again, a group of lads began whistling and shouting at her. She started to run and they chased her.

Poor Gillian ran as fast as she could. She ran passed her friend's address and hoped the gang of boys would go so she could return there.

The mystery was this. Gillian never returned to her friend's flat and no one has seen or heard from her since.

Just imagine how Mr and Mrs Walters felt that morning when they woke up and found out that their beloved daughter was not at home. When she was not with her friends or at school they began to panic.

Gillian's disappearance prompted a massive police hunt in and around the area where she lived.

An elderly woman called Aboulia, who lived on her own in the area, said that she had heard a girl screaming that night. She was inside her house standing near to the window and saw two people look as if they were having a row. A young girl was being pushed by a man.

She told the police that she didn't see who the fellow was because he was wearing a hooded coat that covered his head and disguised his face but after a few minutes the two people went off walking closely together. That was all she saw.

Detective Allan was concerned about the gang of youths that chased Gillian that night so he and a policewoman called Natasha Freeman went and tracked down the five young men who had given her chase and took them to the station for questioning. The boys told the police that they were silly to chase the girl, but they didn't catch up with her and had not seen her again. After the boys had spent many hours at the station, the police confirmed their stories were true and let them go. Soon after that, Natasha began a new investigation. She spent many days questioning Gillian's school friends and her adult friend,

Rosy, who she was going to visit that night. Rosy told the police that she didn't see Gillian that night and she thought that she had changed her mind about coming to see her.

Detective Allan then got to learn that two of Gillian's school friends had a grudge against her and he and Natasha went to find out what that grudge was about and if any of them could be responsible for Gillian disappearance.

'Poor Gillian,' said her friend Jessica with tears in her eyes. She hoped that the police would find her quickly and bring her back to her parents. 'I miss her so much,' said Isobel, another of her school friends.

Rosie got angry with the policewoman for questioning her so much. As soon as the police noticed she had lost her patience they didn't say anything else to her.

By this time many days had past. The police went to see the two schoolgirls they thought were bearing a grudge against Gillian. They told the officers that they had nothing at all to do with Gillian's disappearance.

After many days of investigation the police believed that Gillian might not have been murdered but abducted to another country.

Gillian's broken-hearted parents made several appeals to those who might have abducted their daughter, but they didn't receive any ransom letters or telephone calls about their missing daughter.

All that Gillian's parents and friends could do was wait and hope that the police would find Gillian soon and bring her home alive. Until then the search for Gillian Walters continued.

CHAPTER 7

THE POLICE BLOCKADE

One morning two weeks later, just as Jeremy and Sally were about to go for a stroll, he had a call from Detective Doctor Whoot. He should go and meet Sergeant Collin at a police blockade, barely half a mile away from Jeremy's home. Within a few minutes Jeremy and his wife came to the scene. There were many police officers at the cordoned off High Street, but Officer Collin wasn't there yet.

In this large multicultural area most of the residents lived in back-to-back houses. Their children had very little space in which to play and most of the time they would play ball in the street or go to the local park which, that day, the police had blocked off. They had also cordoned off a stretch of houses in the area near the local park and only the residents who lived in the street were allowed to go home if they were out before the blockade.

It had been reported to the police that certain people were coming to the area under cover of darkness to abuse the poor, young and innocent girls in the area. 'Some, red light district,' they said.

The residents didn't know this at the time but that wasn't the real reason the police were there. They had received a call in the early morning that human remains had been discovered beneath floorboards in one of the houses near the local park.

As Jeremy's wife, Sally, stood there waiting for Sergeant Collin to arrive at the scene she saw something unusual and gave her husband a nudge.

'Jeremy, look.'

He saw many police officers in disguise driving unofficial vehicles; one had a hydraulic lifting system, pretending to be road maintenance engineers repairing streetlights. Then suddenly and unexpectedly a drama began. The officers put their plan into action and broke into one of the houses at the front of the park.

Within 20 minutes or so they came out, each of them wearing facemasks and with oxygen on their backs. By this time word must have got out that the police had found a missing schoolgirl's remains beneath the floorboards and a large crowd of onlookers were gathered at the scene. The officers who came out of the building were quite surprised to see the growing crowd of people.

Shortly after, an officer reported the crime to her superior in Manchester.

Speaking from her radio car she told the officer that the killer had escaped the police blockade but they had apprehended his girlfriend. She described a young girl who had being missing from home a long time ago. It could have been her body that had been found in the house.

By this time the officers who had entered the suspect's house couldn't be sure if the victim they had found was the body of the missing girl or not.

Sergeant Collins asked the police officers to move the crowd back. He was furious that so many officers were at the scene, yet the suspect had been able to escape.

Detective Collins thought that the dead girl might have been hidden there by the Cruel Four gang some time ago.

Later in the day Detective Collins spoke to a newspaper editor. 'Please keep the story out of the papers,' he asked. He didn't want to drive the rest of the gang further underground.

After he had finished talking to the editor he asked his officers to go and strengthen the blockade. Nobody was allowed to enter or leave the surrounded area. Then the people heard that the murderer had escaped and in protest they wanted to take control of the situation, but the police didn't allow them to enter the surrounding area, so they began shouting, 'Let's kill the killer.'

Seeing the crowd trying to take control, the police turned up in force and the crowd gradually drifted away.

Back at the scene Detective Collins asked all the officers who had entered the suspect's house to make a report to him. When they returned with their reports Detective Collins wasn't in the office so they gave them to Jeremy.

The female officer who had discovered the suspect's girlfriend described her. She was white with a dark complexion, thinly built of medium height, about 25 years old.

After Detective Collins had read the statements about the suspect's girlfriend he called two of his female officers, Tracy and Emily, and sent them to the suspect's home to arrest and bring her to the station for questioning.

When the officers went to the house to arrest the woman there was only a small number of angry people left at the scene. As soon as they brought the suspect's girlfriend outside some people began shouting abuse at her. She looked extremely distressed and the people thought she had lost her mind.

'I am so confused! She cried while looking at the people shouting abuse at her.

Then a passing stranger shouted at her, 'Woman, just think you're all on your own now.' She turned sad eyes and looked at the stranger.

'Madam,' an officer said, 'you'll have to tell the detective where your boyfriend has gone, won't you?' She didn't reply to the officer's remarks. They took her away in the police car to the station and into a room for questioning.

As soon as she sat down Jeremy turned sharply and looked at her. 'I am the crime fighter Jeremy Ashman and this is Detective Emily Manson. Can you tell us your name and age?'

'My name is Angelina Winters, I am 24 years old.'

Detective Manson said 'Do you have any children?'

'No.'

The officer continued, 'How long have you been a resident at your present address?'

"Just over two years now,' she said.

As soon as she said this, officer Manson looked at Jeremy. The girl's body had been hidden there over three years. Officer Manson continued, 'So where did you live before?'

'At my parents and she gave their name and address.

'How old is your boyfriend, what is his name and how long has he been living with you? Has he lived there over the same period of time?'

'Oh, no,' she replied, 'Harry, I only met him about a year ago.'

As soon as she said this officer Manson looked at Jeremy again, as the crime had been committed before the suspect went to live there. So, another murderer could be out there somewhere.

Jeremy said, 'Can you tell us how the skeleton was discovered?'

She answered through tears, 'It was the workmen who came to repair the floorboards and discovered her wrapped in black plastic bags.'

Jeremy continued, 'Did Harry ever get upset with you or attempt to kill you? When he went out at night did he tell you where he was going or offer to take you with him?'

'Yes,' she said, 'he took me out with him once or twice.'

'When you and he had a disagreement did he at any time tell you that he was going to kill you?' Jeremy said.

'We've had our ups and down at times, but he's never said that.'

'Well,' Jeremy said, 'whenever he's taken you out where did you go?'

'Sometimes he'd take me for a meal and other times to a local pub.'

Jeremy continued, 'Did his friends ever come to visit him at your home?'

'Oh, no,' she said, 'he told me that he had three best friends but he never brought them to the house or tell me their names.'

'Did he ever tell you the name of his parents and did you ever ask him about them?'

'He didn't wish to tell me about them so I did not need to ask.'

'Do you know that he's been killing young girls, girls even younger than you and hiding their bodies?' Detective Manson said, 'some of which haven't been discovered?'

As soon as she heard this she began crying. Speaking through her tears she said, 'I had no idea he was a murderer. If he was killing people I didn't know of it. Why does everybody hate me? I have never killed anyone.'

As soon as she said this her solicitor John Ackerman came in. After he had read her statement she was allowed to go home. If her boyfriend was to get in touch with her she should tell Detective Manson straight away. She left the station but couldn't return to her house as it was under police investigation. The police released her as the murder was committed at the house before she and the suspect went to live there. Following a new investigation the police went back to the scene of crime where many police officers were waiting. Some of them were hiding in trees near the house to see if any of the suspect's friends came to visit. As the officers looked on, a boy and his dog came into the restricted area.

'Officer William,' one officer shouted, 'please go and stops that lad and his dog.'

'Young man,' he shouted, 'you're not allowed in the restricted area.'

Then another officer had second thoughts as the boy might live in the area or just sneaked through the police barrier.

While Officer William was talking to the boy a lady who lived at the other side of the road opened a window and shouted, 'Charlie, was it you who came from London the other day to help the police in their enquiry about the missing girl?'

But the police replied, 'Madam, Charlie can't speak with you now, he'll have to leave this area.'

As soon as the officer said this, the lady shut her window and went back inside. As the day wore on none of the suspect's friends visited the house so the blockade of the area was ended and the police decided to extend their search for the suspect.

Some officers thought the killer might try to leave the country so they kept a close watch at the airports and the train stations. After the police had lifted the blockade the crowd of onlookers drifted away.

Six months passed and it seemed that the police had completely lost track of the suspect. The peoples' fear grew stronger as they didn't know when or where the killer might strike again

CHAPTER 8

THE BUTCHER'S SHOP

Jeremy's thoughts went back to 30 March 1984 when he and his wife Sally went for a stroll on the other side of the city. They were looking for new accommodation in a quiet place.

As they were driving along the Kirkstall Road that led towards the airport Sally saw a butcher's shop with a sign 'Flat for Sale.'

She looked at her husband, 'We might be in luck.'

Jeremy took a look, parked the jeep and taking his wife by the hand they went into the shop to enquire about the property. As they walked in they saw three people – a white male and a white female at the counter and a black male who was seated on a stool talking to them.

The lady met them with a big smile on her face and the black guy got up from his seat and took off his hat to say hello to Sally. Jeremy looked at his wife and she looked at him, thinking, 'Hopefully, the flat is still available for sale', as it seemed a friendly neighbourhood. She approached the counter to chat with the young lady who worked there.

Jeremy stood looking at the black man seated on the stool and he was almost sure it was the same man he'd seen at Mr Harris's home three days after Christmas 1977, digging a shallow grave in the backyard. He had no doubt he was a member of the Cruel Four.

Jeremy also noticed that the suspect was wearing the same black felt hat and pair of black leather gloves he was wearing that day. Not surprisingly, when he saw the guy he turned his face away so as not to be recognised.

Then things began to heat up. The butcher said to Sally, 'Lady how can I be of help?' in an unfriendly tone of voice. Sally looked him in the eyes and knew from that very minute that the butcher looked at her hatefully and didn't share her smile.

'Well...' Sally said in a rambling voice. She was quite astonished at the butcher's behaviour.

'We've come to look at the flat you have for sale.'

The butcher was quite unfriendly with her again and the woman spoke up to say, 'Why are you being so rude to the lady?'

Then she turned to Sally, 'I've never seen him behave in such a way before.'

Instead of telling Sally about the flat the butcher began to describe the weekly takings of the business to her. As she was talking with the butcher, the guy who they suspected to be a member of the Cruel Four gang began to leave.

He got off the stool and took a sly look at the butcher's girl saying, 'Don't forget the new order that is coming this afternoon – for the seven fresh chickens.'

After he said this he smiled as if it was only a joke. As he spoke, the butcher took a red knife and ripped through the abdomen of one of the chickens he had on sale and the chicken splattered on the floor in front of Sally who, being weak-hearted, immediately fainted and fell lifeless to the floor.

Jeremy kept his cool, but struggled with his wife as he tried to wake her up.

At the same time as the suspect was leaving the shop he saw Jeremy struggling with his wife but didn't offer a helping hand. Instead he looked back at the butcher and said, 'Seeing that you've ripped through the bird in such a way it reminded me that I have a date tonight with a young chick.'

As soon as he said that the butcher's girl got annoyed.

'Guy,' she shouted aloud 'you're always dating others, what about me?'

After she said this, the guy popped his head back through the door saying, 'I'll date whosoever I please. Why don't you try doing the same?' Then he paused and went on his way.

He went off walking towards the city and turned off into a park with a letter in his hand. It was to hide at the root of a tree for his next victim.

By this time, Jeremy struggled with his wife until he got her out of the shop and onto the side of the road where she regained consciousness and opened her eyes.

'Thank God,' Jeremy said. 'Sally, you're back with us again, are you okay?'

'Yes,' she replied, what has happened?'

As he was trying to help her to the jeep he spotted the reflection of the butcher coming towards them with his knife hidden behind his back. When Jeremy said he had called the police he changed his mind.

After the butcher went back into the shop Jeremy asked Detective Mullins to send some of his men to keep a watch on the black guy as he might be a member of the Cruel Four gang.

Now that Sally had regained her composure she remembered seeing the guy with the letter in his hand when she had first entered the shop.

Jeremy had intended to wait until the Detective's men arrived but seeing his wife standing on wobbly knees he got her into the jeep to take her home.

It was late afternoon in the peak hours. When they were on their way home and passing the Town Hall, Sally asked Jeremy to stop and tell the police about the butcher and the guy who had hidden the letter in the park to trap his next victim. But the road was busy so they carried on driving home.

As Sally was getting out of the jeep her legs gave way and she almost fell to the ground.

'Please,' she cried, 'help me up and out of the way.'

She was afraid of a car coming the opposite way she was so unsteady on her feet.

Then a passing stranger heard her cry and came to her saying, 'I'll help you, madam.'

'Thank you very much,' Jeremy said, 'I will see to her from here.'

As he was carrying Sally to the house the stranger followed, entered the house, stood in the passageway and leaned on the wall.

He looked sharply at Jeremy saying, 'You should have known that your wife wasn't strong enough and got hold of her before she fell.'

Jeremy wondered where this nosey stranger had come from and why was he jumping to conclusions? He passed the stranger in the passageway, took his wife into the living room and went to the stranger.

'Thank you very much, but you can go now – a doctor is coming to see my wife.'

'That's a good idea, the stranger said, and stood in the passageway near the door so it couldn't close.

'Sir,' Jeremy uttered, 'will you please get on your way?'

'I will not go,' the stranger said, 'I'll just stick around until this whole affair is over.'

'What affair?' Jeremy asked astonished. 'What are you are talking about?'

Instead of replying the stranger went past him and stood again in the passageway.

Jeremy began thinking, 'Who does this stranger think he is? And what does he know about me and our private life?'

That moment a car approached the gate and stopped. It was the family doctor who had come to visit Sally.

As soon as the stranger heard that it was the Doctor, was also a private detective he left so fast not even the Doctor was able to talk with him.

The doctor gave Jeremy a prescription for his wife, got into his car and drove away.

CHAPTER 9

THE SUSPECT'S HOUSE

After many days had passed Jeremy looked back to that early morning in May 1983 and remembered he'd promised to meet colleagues at the office.

'Sally,' he shouted, 'I'm going to the office to see a colleague. I'll try not to be late home.'

'Ok,' she answered and gave him a goodbye kiss. As soon as he went through the door he immediately found himself driving along a High Street not very far from home.

As he went on he met two young ladies he'd met once before. They were hanging out with some older guys who had been arrested for the possession of some illegal substances.

As soon as the two girls saw Jeremy they ran to his car. As they approached him one said, 'Hi, Mr,' with a big smile on her face. The other girl said, 'We don't even know your name.'

'Well, Jeremy muttered, 'so, we meet again!'

'Yes,' the older girl spoke bravely.

Jeremy looked at the younger of the two. 'So, what's your name then?'

'I am Judith Mosley,' she said. 'And I'm Coral Kay,' said the other girl

Jeremy stretched his hand to them saying, 'I'm Jeremy Ashman. Good to see you again!'

Then one of the girls whispered to her friend so that Jeremy couldn't hear.

Then Jeremy said, 'Look, I have to go so can you tell me how I can be of help?'

As soon as he said this the girls looked at each other as of to ask which of them should talk first.

Jeremy looked at Judith. 'How old are you?' he asked.

'I'm 15,' she said, 'and my friend is 16.'

'What do your parents think when they see you standing around on a street corner like this? Don't they care?'

'Our parents are dead,' said Judith.

'Dead,' Jeremy repeated. 'Are you sisters?'

'No, said Coral, we come from the same care home.'

'Where is that?' he asked. 'How long ago did you run away from there? Are you going to school? If so, which one?'

'We're not telling you,' said the oldest girl. 'We've left the care home to live on our own.'

'Who is looking after you now?' He asked.

'We have boyfriends,' Coral replied. 'Don't we, Judith?'

'Yes,' she replied.

Then the older of the two said, 'We just wanted to tell you that my friend and I may know a guy who might have kidnapped the girl the police are looking for.'

'Do you now?' Jeremy spoke with doubt. He was unconvinced, because he could tell that one of the girls was filling with jealousy. Her boyfriend was dating another girl. Jeremy looked at her again, 'Is this why you are resentful of your boyfriend? If you know he is the kidnapper why not tell the police?'

As soon as he mentioned the police she became reluctant to say anything else.

Jeremy knew quite well that the girls couldn't be trusted because they had lied to him before. He didn't expect them to be telling the truth. However, he decided to follow them to the house just to see what the boyfriend was up to. He parked his car at the side of the avenue.

He didn't trust the girls and kept a safe distance behind them. He thought they might betray him and lead him into a trap. The fact remained that he was looking for the missing schoolgirl, Gillian Walters and this could be his first lead in the investigation.

As they were walking, the girls took a short cut that lead to a back road that had no name. Jeremy took out his notebook, made a note of the place and continued walking slowly behind the two girls. He tried to keep a safe distance until they got to the house.

Before they arrived at the suspect's house, Jeremy picked up another clue: he noticed that the house where they were going didn't have a number. So he took out his notebook again and wrote down, 'a house without a number, on a road that has no name.'

He began to weigh up the situation and his mind became confused. His heart began to beat faster.

Then to add more to an uncomfortable situation, as the girls reached the house they stopped, chatted, looked back towards him and giggled.

After seeing this he slowed down and dropped back further behind.

They went on a little further and parted company. The youngest girl went to a house, which was not far from that of her friend.

Before she went through the door she stuck two fingers up and gave Jeremy a wave with the victory sign. Perhaps this was her way of saying goodbye.

Now that one of the girls had gone, the other looked back at Jeremy who was walking slowly now a fair distance behind.

'Hurry up,' she said, using her hand instead of her voice.

Jeremy ran on to catch up with her.

'Are you sure this is the right house where the guy lives?'

'Yes,' she answered.

'Well,' Jeremy uttered, 'do you think he's at home now with the girl he's kidnapped?'

Instead of replying she looked at Jeremy and put her finger up to her mouth, motioning him to be quiet. Perhaps she wanted to give the guy a surprise visit. As they arrived at the house Jeremy decided to wait outside the back door just in case the man became aggressive. He allowed the girl to go inside. She left the door unlocked in case she had to come out again in a rush. As soon as she went inside the house, a dog started barking. The guy must have heard the dog barking, looked outside and saw Jeremy waiting. He got angry and shut the door.

'Who is that man you've brought home with you?'

Before the girl was able to reply, he got hold of her and twisted her arm.

'You're hurting me!' she cried out aloud so that Jeremy could hear from outside.

When Jeremy heard the girl crying, he went to the house and tried the door but it was locked so he took a peep through the window. He could have panicked. He recognised the guy as a member of the Cruel Four gang who had escaped from the police some time ago. When the guy looked and saw him looking through the window he immediately got hold of the girl and forced her to kiss him. Then he pointed to the door and shouted at Jeremy saying, 'Keep off number 48, or else.'

Jeremy began weighing up the situation in his mind. Could it have been the same guy who took the number 48 from the house door and left the road without a name?

He began to picture him in his mind as a white male, of medium build and just under than six feet tall. The two girls were young enough to be his daughters.

The suspect let go of the girl and she went into the passageway where the dog was tied up. Now that the back door was locked Jeremy would have to run all the way round a block of houses if he wanted to enter

Despite being terrified of passing the dog he decided to go in and help the girl. He didn't hear the guy shout out, 'If anybody tells the police, they will never see the girl again.'

CHAPTER 10

THE MISSING SCREWS

As Jeremy was running to the front of the house, the suspect changed his clothes. When Jeremy had first seen him he was wearing a shirt and trousers but when Jeremy got to the front of the building the guy had pulled a trick on him and went across the main road. At the side of the road a street light pole was bolted down with four screws. The guy removed three of the screws that left the street light pole leaning dangerously towards the main road.

When he looked and saw Jeremy coming towards the main road he pretended to be struggling to hoist up the street light pole on his own.

'Help!' he cried out.

Jeremy didn't recognise that it was the bad guy so ran to give him a helping hand. As soon as he got hold of the street light pole to help, he let go of it and showed Jeremy the three screws he had taken out saying, 'Until these screws are found the street light pole shall remain leaning.'

This was an analogy but he was actually saying that until all members of the Cruel Four gang were caught and in prison,

Jeremy's story would always be considered a fabrication. As soon as he said this he left, leaving Jeremy alone holding up the street light pole, crying out for help, but nobody would listen to him. At length help came and Jeremy was free and he went back to the suspect's house, by which time they had all gone and left the dog still tied up in the passageway.

Jeremy had a look around the inside of the house to see if he could pick up any clues as to where they could have gone. He found a few bits of paper that looked like shipping labels. One scrap of paper had South Africa written on it but no address. He searched some more until he came upon some other bits of letters that suggested they could have fled to the West Indies by plane.

The question was this, had he taken the two girls with him? With all these thoughts Jeremy went immediately to the house where the younger girl lived, but nobody was there. So he went back to the suspect's house, untied the dog to see where it went, so he might follow.

'Poor dog,' he said and gave it a stroke.

It seemed very calm even though its owner had left it behind and tied with a string. Jeremy hoped that he might find some solid proof in the house then he would report the situation to Detective Doctor Whoot but he didn't find any. As soon as he unchained the dog it immediately shot off, leaving him to wonder where it had gone.

After a long search to find the girls Jeremy went home tired. After explaining the situation to his wife it was time for bed. He was just about to get into bed when the phone rang. Sally picked up the phone, handed it to him saying, 'It's a woman named Judith. She says that it's urgent'.

'My God,' he uttered, 'I thought that she had been kidnapped and taken by the Cruel Four. Judith,' he said, 'where are you?'

She gave him directions to where she and her friend were in hiding. Jeremy didn't hesitate, took his jeep and off he went. Following Judith's instructions he came to a location on the outskirts of the city. He flashed the headlights twice and the two young ladies came out of hiding.

The one of them named Coral said, 'Jeremy we are scared'.

Jeremy said, 'I thought that the guy had taken you two away with him, how did you manage to escape?'

Coral said, 'While you were running around the block of houses to get to the front he went out through the front door to a street light across the main road. And I went and got my friend and we ran away from him and hid ourselves here. Now we can't go back to our place because he might kill us.'

'Do not worry,' Jeremy said, 'I went to the house and nobody was there – just the dog tied up in the passageway'.

'Yes,' she said, 'we didn't have enough time to let the dog loose. Now we may not find our Spotty because we haven't anywhere to go where the guy can't find us. I want my dog,' she cried.

'Well,' Jeremy said, 'your dog is at the office. If you decide to change your lifestyle we can arrange a safe home for you and your friend and then you might have your dog back. And someone will be there to look after you and help you to educate yourself and to become respectable ladies instead of working for pimps. However, if you refuse to go to the safe home we'll arrest you for unlawful acts in the street. The ball is in your court'.

As soon as he said this, Judith looked at Coral, 'What do you reckon?' she asked.

Coral nodded her head. 'Yes.'

"Coral,' Jeremy spoke, 'tell me something about the guy who's your boyfriend. What's his name?'

Coral said, 'Sometimes he's Tam and sometimes he's something else. He never gives us his right name.'

'Well,' Jeremy continued, 'did he at any time mention he might be going to South America or to South Africa or to the West Indies?'

'Yes,' she said, 'if he was going abroad I guess that he would most likely go to the West Indies or South Africa.'

But she didn't think that he would leave for another country without taking them with him. Two policewomen then came from the Detective's office to collect the girls. Detective Mulling had also sent some officers to secure the houses where the girls used to stay.

Before they were taken away Jeremy shouted to one of the officers, 'Kelsey may I have a word in private please?'

'Of course,' she replied, 'how can I help?'

'I just want to say that when the girls settle down at their safe home you can give the dog back to them. And please can you make some inquiries? Find out which care home the girls were at before they ran away and if any of them were reported missing at the time.'

Jeremy knew perfectly well that someone would have an account of the ill-treatment of these young girls.

Jeremy also asked if she could find out which school the girls used to go to and if they had any relatives.

'Is that all sir?' she asked.

'Yes,' he said, 'for the moment.'

And they took the girls with them and drove away.

CHAPTER 11

A TRIP TO THE WEST INDIES

Two weeks after the member of the Cruel Four gang went into hiding Detective Doctor Whoot called a meeting with his men. He thought that the guy known as Tam might have gone to the West Indies to hide from the police.

Jeremy had also suggested that it might be the same man who had kidnapped Gillian Walters. Michael Felix, one of the detectives, said, 'Why would Tam ship his belongings to South Africa and South America and then go went to the West Indies?'

As soon as he said this Detective Doctor Whoot came to an immediate decision saying, 'Jeremy, you're going to the West Indies to see what you can find out about the runaway known as Tam'.

Then he looked at Michael and said, 'And you're going to South Africa and to see what you can find out about the same man'.

So Jeremy found himself in the West Indies, searching for the serial killer and the girl who he might have kidnapped named Gillian Walters. It was suspected that he might be hiding her somewhere in one of three villages.

CHAPTER 12

SOUTH AFRICA

In South Africa Detective Michael Felix woke up in the early morning and as the day wore on went from his hotel for a stroll in the village. As he was on his way towards the village to search for the suspect he heard a man's voice shout, 'Mister!' He stopped and waited to see what the person wanted him for.

A middle-aged man approached him crying.

'What on earth is the matter with you?' he asked the man.

The man was too upset and couldn't answer straight away so he asked him to sit down at the side of the dirt road. The man leaned forward, rested his head in his hands and cried some more.

'Do you have a name?' Michael asked. 'Are you a native of South Africa?'

'No, it's about my son, who left Poland and went to Great Britain to visit me on 6 June, three years ago, but before he got to my home he was kidnapped by a group of men who took him to South Africa. Now he's here in a secret jail crying out that freedom will never come for him.'

After he said this, Michael put his finger up to his mouth for a moment to think.

While they were seated at the side of the dirt road under a cloudless sky Michael began thinking about what the stranger said about his son being kidnapped. Then he turned and looked at the stranger, 'Why didn't you report your missing son to the British police?'

Instead of replying to the question the stranger gave Michael, his name.

'I'm Mick, he said, 'I come from Poland but I've lived in Great Britain for a long time now. I came to South Africa to find my son.'

After he said this he paused with a sad look on his face and a trickle of tears fell from his eyes.

Michael said, 'Mick, shouldn't you report this to the South Africa authorities and find out why your son is in prison in their country?'

As soon as Michael said this, Mick broke down again and started to cry.

Michael thought that Mick and his son might be involved in something much greater than they were able to handle. Were they in some kind of trouble with the South African government and not telling him the truth?

'Mick I was just thinking that your son might not have been kidnapped from Britain as you say. Has he been arrested by the South Africa secret police?'

'Nonsense,' he replied angrily. 'I told you that I come from Poland but I've lived in Great Britain now for a long time.'

'But this is South Africa,' Michael said, 'don't you agree?'

Mick turned his head away and started to sob again.

Michael didn't know if Mick was telling him the truth, but he noticed that he was wearing a crumpled suit as if he was drinking hard and sleeping rough.

Michael stood and waited until Mick dried his tears and started to talk again. He began by describing the secret jail in which his son was being kept against his will.

In spite of all the sympathy Michael might have had for Mick and his son, he wasn't able to help him free his son in that way.

Michael looked at Mick and could see he was devastated to see someone from Great Britain with whom he could share his sorrow.

'Mick, can I ask you a question?' said Michael.

'Sure,' he replied.

'Well,' Michael declared, 'if your son was kidnapped and taken to South Africa three years ago in June 1984, why are you crying now?'

'I told you already,' he said, 'nobody will believe my story, not even the police.'

As soon as he said this, Michael noticed that whenever Mick spoke of his missing son he had a certain strain of bitterness in his heart that may never vanish from his mind.

CHAPTER 13

THE SECRET JAIL

Mick looked at Michael saying, 'I'm crying tears of joy because after all these years. At long last I've found out he's still alive!'

Michael now realised why Mick was so glad to see him – he thought Michael would help him break his son out of South Africa's well-guarded jail.

Michael thought how in this God's world could he and Mick work single-handedly to break his son out of a well-guarded jail? Even if Mick's son was innocent, his father's idea about rescuing him was ludicrous. However, Mick thought that whatever the cost he was not leaving his son.

Now from one word to another Mick became impatient with Michael. 'Are you going to help me? He asks, Yes or no?'

Michael looked at him, 'Mick, dry up your tears and act like a man and then I'll see what I can do to help.'

'I'm sorry,' Mick said, 'it's just the heaviness in my heart that keeps bringing tears to my eyes.'

Next day Mick got up early and went with Michael to look over the jail.

'I'll lead the way, all you have to do is follow me,' said Mick.

After about three miles they bumped into a man with an old rusty open back truck who was willing to show them a quicker way to get to the jail at a price. But when Michael looked at the old truck, he said, 'Is he going to drive us there in that?'

'Pretty much so,' the driver said, 'pretty much so.'

'Well,' Michael said, I would rather walk than to drive in that old truck.'

'Ok then, Mick said, 'we can walk it from here – it isn't too far now.'

As they were walking along a narrow country path they met some native people who showed them a shorter way to get to the prison. Mick and Michael went on walking. The dirt road led through beautiful countryside and the landscapes were breathtaking. Animals ran all around and it was most exciting. After they had walked for several more miles they caught sight of a large common with barbed wire fencing around it.

As soon as Mick saw this he lifted his hand to Michael, 'This is it, keep your head low.'

Michael looked at Mick and a smile appeared on his face – probably for the first time in the three years his son had been missing.

'Are you quite sure this is the place?' Michael asked.

'Of course,' he said, 'I'm very sure.' Then he lengthened his stride and went closer to the common. 'I've waited three long years for this moment!'

Michael gazed up at the high fencing which looked dangerous to climb. After they had examined the situation carefully, Mick decided that he would climb over the fencing alone and Michael would watch out for him. He stood looking at the fencing before climbing over into the common for a better view.

Mick thought that if he went into the common he would be able to see what was on the other side. Mick should have thanked his lucky stars when, just as he was about to put his hand on the wire fencing, they heard a girl's voice cry out, 'Mister! Do not touch those fences!'

'Christ!' Michael cried out astonished.

The young lady had just saved Mick's life. The fencing he was about to hold on to was electrified.

After the young lady told him of the danger he stood there, frightened out of his wits.

CHAPTER 14

BISHOP WASN'T A PREACHER

Back in the West Indies Jeremy spent some hours in a small village surrounded by plantations. Then he went for a stroll but wasn't sure whereabouts on the island he was. As he was heading through the village another emergency arose. Detective Doctor Whoot had given him a new and urgent assignment.

He was told to search and find a man called Bishop because he and his family were in immediate danger of being assassinated.

It had come to light that a group of corrupt people were secretly planning to assassinate Bishop and his family and take over his position. They were plotting to take over the government of the island but Jeremy wasn't aware of this at the time.

There wasn't much time to search and find Bishop and warn him of the deadly plot against him and his family. Jeremy stood as one who was lost in wonder. He didn't have a clue as to where Bishop could be found and time was running out. He went from one village to another; hopefully somebody might know where he lived. Jeremy thought that Bishop could be a preacher and his thoughts went back to Britain and his home in Yorkshire.

That night before he left home Sally had told him she was taking the children with her on holiday to Blackpool while he was away. At the time she was upstairs making the children's beds and he was downstairs with the children. She shouted from upstairs, 'Children it's time for bed.'

Then she shouted to her young son, Isaac, 'you and Naomi say goodnight to your Dad and come on up to bed, or else!'

She hadn't made up her mind what punishment to give if the children disobeyed her. However, Isaac put on a sad face and said goodnight to Billy his pet budgie, hugged his Dad and said 'goodnight.'

His sister, Naomi, likewise gave her pet fish a kiss from the outside of the tank saying, 'Goodnight Goldie!' The fish began acting as if it knew that Naomi was going to bed and wanted to follow her and began swimming around in the tank.

Meanwhile back in the West Indies Jeremy continued until he came to another village. As soon as he entered the district he heard the sound of music coming from the city parade, which was some distance away from the actual town. The village was extremely green and the place was beautiful.

The wind was fresh and the sky was blue. More beauty was added by the many citrus trees, with colourful fruit along the side of the road that lead towards the town. Jeremy looked towards the distant fields where he saw fruit trees that looked like beautiful flowers hanging down towards the ground.

He continued towards the town and came upon two native teenage boys, 'Hello,' he shouted. One of the young men gave heed.

'Are you talking to us?' he asked.

'Yes' Jeremy said, 'can you please tell me if there is a Bishop living anywhere in this area?'

The boys looked at each other. Then one of them called Jeremy, 'Mister, you might have come to the wrong village. There isn't a Bishop who lives round here.'

The other boy said, 'If you go back to the main road over there,' he pointed, 'you can ask again.'

'Ok,' Jeremy said, 'thank you very much!'

Then he looked around and said out loud, 'It's getting hot already!'

The boy overheard him and said, 'Yeah man, it does get hot at this time of the year.'

After saying this Jeremy headed back toward the main road as directed. He was overwhelmed at the beautiful countryside but couldn't forget how urgent the situation was. A cold wind began to blow off the sea, which wasn't far from where he was.

As he was going towards the main road he met an elderly woman carrying her bags of shopping towards the bus stop. He made several attempts to cross the road but there was too much traffic. Farmers rode their saddled mules at speed through the scorching hot sun. Perhaps they were taking their products to the market to sell.

Jeremy was excited at the beautiful scene and almost forgot how urgent his mission was. He was running out of time to warn Bishop of the imminent danger.

Then he looked at the time. 'Oh, no,' he cried out.

The day was almost spent. He looked at his watch again and jotted down the date in the middle of his hand – 21 June 1983.

While he was trying to cross the road again he bumped into some more native people.

'Excuse me, please,' he uttered, 'can any of you nice people tell me if a man called Bishop lives anywhere around here?'

One of the strangers looked at the other who said, 'the only Bishop we know who lives round here is Bishop the President.'

Jeremy looked at the strangers with frightened eyes, 'Is Bishop a President?' he asked in a nervous tone of voice.

'Yes,' replied the stranger, 'he's the only Bishop that we know who lives here.'

Then one of the ladies pointed a finger towards the palace saying, 'He lives just a little further up the road, you can't miss it.'

As soon as she said this Jeremy's heart went with a leap as he thought that someone was going to assassinate the President.

CHAPTER 15

THE TOP SECURITY PRISON

Back in South Africa Michael and Mick didn't see the girl who had told him not to touch the electric fencing. He stood still on the spot until he had regained his composure and shouted, 'Whoever you may be, thank you very much for saving my life.'

Then they saw a beautiful young Chinese girl with very long dark hair suddenly appear from behind a large tree on the common.

She was about 16 years old. Mick looked at her, 'Young lady,' he said, 'thank you very much. You have just saved me and my friend's lives.'

The girl gave her name as Yung.

'Please Yung,' Mick appealed to the girl, 'can you tell us if you at any time you have seen such person as I described?'

Instead of replying Yung began to cry and lots of tears ran down her face. Then she regained her composure and began to speak through her tears. 'We are all freedom fighters in prison – we'll never get out of here.'

As soon as she said this, Mick stood frozen for a while waiting to hear what the young lady was going to say about his son. But she turned with frightened eyes and looked at the large tree in the common as if someone was there listening to what she had to say.

'Miss Yung,' Michael spoke, can I ask you a question?'

She nodded her head.

'What are they keeping you in prison for?'

'They think I am one of the freedom fighters and have kept me here to be their cook. We are well cared for, but freedom will never come for us.'

'Is that so?' Mick spoke angrily. 'Young lady I'll bring you freedom now. Please do not move; I'll only be a minute. He went and found a pick and a shovel. Then he returned.
'I'll have you out of there in no time.'

As soon as he said this, Yung cried out fearfully and pointed towards the large tree in the common.

'They will always see you first.'

Michael looked up into the tree saw a full range of spy equipment; hidden there was a large camera combined with television and laser-powered guns attached, ready to shoot at any intruders.

As soon as Mick was putting his plan into action to rescue the girl they heard horses galloping.

The girl shouted out, 'The solders are coming on horses!' Then she ran away and hid herself.

By this time the soldiers were just around the corner but Mick was furious, as he didn't want to leave without his son. But Michael got hold of him and pulled him away.

They began running away from the common and just before the soldiers arrived they hid themselves.

'Mick,' Michael uttered, 'come on; let's go before the soldiers find us...'

But Mick was determined not to leave without his son and went berserk.

When they saw how close the soldiers were from catching up to them they started to run. When they were out of sight of the soldiers they stopped running, gasping for breath.

CHAPTER 16

HOLIDAY IN BLACKPOOL

Back in Britain, Sally and her children were in her Jeep heading for Blackpool and later found themselves having a meal at their favourite hotel.

After a few hours at the hotel, Naomi, Sally's daughter cried out, 'Mum guess what? I think we forgot to shut the back door at home!'

'Oh my God,' Sally cried out, knowing very well that their home could be in danger of being burgled.

Then she broke the bad news to the children. 'We'll have to cut short our holiday and return home.'

The children were very sad that they had to leave but they set off for home with their mother. As they were driving from Blackpool on the motorway Sally looked into her mirror and saw an articulated truck coming up behind her at full speed.

She looked at her children and said, 'These large trucks should be driving on their own road.'

She thought that the truck was coming straight at her and the children were very frightened. She looked on, hoping that the truck would overtake instead of driving so close behind them and worried that the truck might be driven by one of the Cruel Four gang.

As she began to panic the truck turned off and went another way. Sally breathed a sigh of relief and the children clinched their fists, 'Yes!'

She drove until they now came to Shipley in Yorkshire by which time it was evening. She drove into a car park at a pub and stopped for her and the children to get something to eat and drink.

The door to enter was already open so they went in. As soon as Sally got in she saw a woman who once was an old friend of hers.

She crept up quietly and gave the woman a nudge on her shoulder saying 'It's been a long time!'

The woman looked at her saying, 'Yes, but you'll have to buy your own.'

Sally's heart dropped as all those stood at the bar turned their eyes and looked at her as if she was scrounging for drinks. Sally's daughter took her hand saying, 'Come on Mummy, let's get out of here.'

However, Sally knew the children were very hungry so she took them to order some food and drink for them, and a glass of milk for herself.

While they were having their meal a group of young girls came into the pub dressed up in a way that could stir up any man's jealousy. The girls were aged between 18 and 25 and there were nine of them.

One of the girls looked at Sally drinking milk and the children with orange juice and nudged her friends who laughed. In a short time the girls were surrounded by men.

The girls were all young and very attractive. Sally had no doubt in her mind that they were a group of call girls looking for clients so decided to take the children and leave. As they were about leave the group of girls got together, had a secret chat and went out before Sally.

Sally and the children went out after them and as they were driving towards Leeds the same articulated lorry started to overtake, so she gave way.

As it was passing by a girl in the truck lifted up a part of the sheet that covered the lorry. Sally was surprised to see the nine young girls from the pub, sat in the truck blindfolded.

Sally shouted out aloud through the window of her Jeep to the girls in the truck, 'Why are you wearing blindfolds?'

The girl in the truck replied, but Sally didn't hear because of the noise of the traffic. She knew that something wasn't right so she tried to read the truck's registration plate.

It was the same as the truck that had passed them on the motorway (61110Y) but she couldn't be sure if she got all of the registration number as the truck turned off and went another way.

Being curious, Sally decided to follow the truck to see where it was taking the nine blindfolded girls. She followed the truck until it came to a large house with a stone wall around it. The truck went through the gate and made its way to the back of the building. Sally couldn't see what they were up to but she believed that the pimps had blindfolded their clients so that they would not be able to find their way back to the house. As soon as Sally discovered the building she turned her Jeep around and drove away.

Next morning Sally reported the incident to Detective Allan and he promised to send some of his men to look into the situation and they put a watch on the house.

Now that Jeremy was involved in another case they also put an undercover watch on Jeremy's home.

A few days passed and nothing happened. Then one night about 2.30 am Detective Colman and his colleague Simon Daily caught sight of a man climbing up onto the roof of Jeremy's home with the intention of breaking in through the skylight window while the family were in bed asleep.

While Sally was in bed a knock came at the door that woke her. She thought that her husband had returned from the West Indies and didn't have a key to get in.

She got out of bed and took a look through the window and her heart dropped with fright. The avenue was filled with police officers and cars. As soon as she opened the door the officers went passed her in a rush and told her that someone was on the roof of her house trying to get in through the skylight window.

As soon as she heard this she and a lady police officer went upstairs and secured the children.

Then they heard officers shout from attic bedrooms 'We got him!'

They handcuffed the criminal and took him to their car. There they found out that they had caught the serial killer.

Would he now tell the police where he had taken young Gillian? And how many people he had already killed and where had he hidden the bodies? One officer thought that this was going to be a long investigation and Detective Doctor Whoot hoped he would tell them where his three colleagues were hiding.

Jeremy was in the West Indies and Michael was still in South Africa when they heard the good news that a member of the Cruel Four gang had been caught and was identified by the two young ladies he had abused.

Michael knew quite well that three of the Cruel Four gang were still on the run so he decided to cut short his assignment and return home as quickly as possible.

CHAPTER 17

THE ASSASSIN

Back in the West Indies, Jeremy continued with his assignment he's now arrived at the President's palace gate. He stood for a moment and looked around the place but couldn't see anybody. He went a little closer towards the highly cultivated land that had many beautiful flowers around the gardens. The lawn was most extravagant. He was surprised there weren't any soldier's on guard duty or any sign of the President's cars.

Jeremy was in two minds if it was safe for him to enter without an invitation. At this point it seemed as if nothing serious had happened. The entrance to the palace door was partly open and his heart sank. Maybe the assassins had already done their job?

Then to his horror, he took a fearful look inside but nobody was to be seen. So he went in on tiptoes to look around. As soon as he went into the hall the door that he came through suddenly slammed shut behind him. Had he walked into a trap? He went looking for a way to get back out of the building. A passageway that led further into the palace was open. He went in with watchful eyes. On each side of the passageway there were beautiful rooms.

He could only see the inside by looking through the windows but sadly there was nobody in any of the rooms and his heart began beating faster.

Things didn't seem right. Had he left it too late? He became scared at being a stranger walking through the President's palace. He didn't know what to expect. If there was another way to get out of the building, he didn't know of it.

He saw an open door but before he could get there the door slammed and locked itself solid. Jeremy became more and more curious. He hadn't found the President or seen any of his people in the palace. Now he himself was in a trap.

'My God!' he cried, 'how am I going to get out of here?'

He thought that by this time the President and his staff may have already been assassinated and as he was searching for a way to escape he found himself in another room filled with luxury things.

It seemed as if the whole building had been recently abandoned and he was trapped in one of the rooms. He shouted, 'Hello – is anybody here?' but there was no reply.

He looked at the window and saw the West Indies sun sending a sparkling glaze of lights through the trees and reflection inside the room. He thought of climbing to the roof but that was too risky. Then he began thinking that he had found himself in a very dangerous situation that he wasn't able to handle alone.

'What am I going to do now?' He panicked more and more. Then he began to have a revelation. He was aware in a strange way of a message: that the assassin was already inside the President quarters, hiding behind long purple curtains, waiting to pounce on the President when he entered the room.

Jeremy considered that the President might have become an enemy to someone who was now hatching a secret plot to assassinate him, his family and friends. Then they would take over his position by force.

On the other hand, the assassin could have come from Cuba or from Russia or even another part of the West Indies. At this point, there wasn't an immediate explanation for this deadly plot.

The only possible way of gaining access to the President's quarters was to climb out of one of the bedrooms, which would be highly dangerous.

He took a look up and saw a narrow gap close to the roof. He climbed with difficulty. Eventually he got to the top and forced his way through and landed in the next apartment.

Thankfully, there were carpets on the floor or else he would have surely hurt himself. From here, he was able to see the President. He was just leaving his sitting room, going to lunch with his family and men.

This was the only opportunity he had to see the President but he couldn't get any closer to him. When the President went to dine, a group of armed men went into his apartment and hid behind the long purple curtains where they waited to attack him when he returned.

By this time Jeremy had tried every way possible to alert the President of the danger but he couldn't get his attention, so there was nothing he could do to help. At this point it seemed that he was to be the only witness to the crime.

He looked up to the sky in despair as he saw the President innocently walking into the trap. He had a clear view of the

President but just couldn't get the message through to warn him in time. After all the efforts he had made, the President was about to be murdered before his very eyes.

The President had left his devoted men and family behind. They had not realised that the palace had been invaded. When the group of armed men saw the President they waited behind the curtain and didn't make a sound. They allowed him to come inside and sit down in his favourite chair and lean back to relax.

Jeremy couldn't do a thing but only watch the President unwittingly walk into the danger. Again, he wrote down the date on his hand, 21 June, 1983.

After the President sat in his chair and settled down to rest the group of armed men popped out from behind the purple curtain and got hold of him. You can imagine how the President felt, knowing that he had left his security guards behind.

One of the assassins dragged him from the chair saying, 'On your feet!'

The President didn't have any time to fight back. They gave him a terrible blow to his face that made him stagger backwards and fall into his chair again. He felt his chin and looked sharply at the one who'd hit him. He knew then that they had come to kill him.

Jeremy saw this and his heart leaped. He looked and saw a man dressed in presidential clothing, ready to take over when the true President had died. As soon as he came he said, 'Bishop you are a dead man now,' and pointed a gun at his face.

He sent some of his men to search the palace, but the main entrance was closed. Nobody was allowed to enter or leave the building. From the room where Jeremy was locked in he could see and hear all that they were doing, but sadly couldn't do anything to help.

When the group of men decided not to shoot the President Jeremy was glad, as he thought they were going to free him. The President grabbed hold of one of the rebel soldiers but was pushed back into his chair. Then he cried out in pain, 'Should any harm come to my wife and family, you'll all die!'

When the President-to-be heard this he looked sharply at him the man saying, 'Who is going to kill us? You are a dead man,' he paused. And they all began laughing.

'However,' he continued, 'if you are willing to give up and surrender to us peacefully, we'll have no need to kill you.'

The President refused, saying, 'I won't surrender my position to any mob.'

After he said this he grabbed one of the guards who threw him to the ground and hit him until his knees went weak and wobbly. They dragged him to his feet and pushed his face against the glass window so that he could look outside.

There he saw his guardsmen lying dead on the ground and rebels standing in their places. After he saw this, the mob took him away from the window. He was in pain and agony.

Jeremy looked on and his heart began to ache when he heard the chief rebel command his executioners to kill the President. After he had given them the order he went away and left them behind to do the killing.

One of the executioners said to the other, 'Go and fetch me the burning tackle, gas and air.' Jeremy couldn't do anything but looked on in horror as one of the men tested the flame. It could cut through steel in seconds.

Then without compassion for the man, they burnt his face and cut his head and arms and legs clean off.

Jeremy looked on and felt coldness go through his bones. He spontaneously cried out, 'Help!' Some of the soldiers who were outside heard him and came in and looked here and there but Jeremy hid himself so remained undetected.

By this time, the chief of the rebels had sent a group of his bodyguards to see if the President was dead. One of them touched the body with his finger. 'Is he dead?' he asked.

The other looked at him and said, 'Can't you see? They've cut off his head, feet and arms...why ask me if he's dead?'

After the group of men had examined the body they returned and reported to the new President that Bishop was dead.

As soon as he heard this he clenched his fists and punched the air; he was overwhelmed. His wicked plan had worked and it was time to celebrate victory.

Before the old President died he didn't know that when they had invaded his palace they had killed some of his men and captured some others, along with his wife and some devoted members of staff.

The new President arranged a party at the palace to celebrate his predecessor's death. He sent out a car with a loudspeaker to invite hundreds of the local village people to be his guests. When evening came the celebration began. Some of the old President's friends and guards who hadn't been captured didn't know that he had been murdered as they were elsewhere in a secure unit.

As the celebration was in full swing, some of the new President's soldiers took the old President's remains to a burial ground. When they got there the shallow grave had already been dug so they threw the burnt body into the grave, filled it up with dirt and trampled it down with their feet until it was level. Then they went back to the palace to celebrate with the others.

The new President was so excited to know that the old President had died and he and his family took their seats on the balcony with groups of trained guards around them. Everything seemed to be going okay so, the President sat relaxed. The old President was dead and buried – surely there was nothing to be worrying about now.

But while the President and his family were eating and drinking and others were dancing the night away suddenly and unexpectedly the old President popped up before them, headless and without hands or feet, his body rolling on the balcony. But it was only the new President who saw it and he went berserk with fear.

'The headless man is here, will someone shoot it please, don't let it escape!' The President's wife didn't see the headless man but began to scream and their guests stopped dancing and stood still with frightened eyes, wondering what was wrong with them.

The soldiers reached for their guns but they couldn't see anything to shoot at. They thought that the President had being drinking too much.

The old President's body rolled away and disappeared. The new President was terrified and ordered a search party to find the headless body and destroy it.

'Be warned,' he said, 'don't let it return – or else.'

So a group of soldiers went outside and began to search in and around the palace. Tension was running high among the soldiers.

Some of them were afraid that the dead President had returned to take revenge on those who killed him. They searched the area thoroughly and in the palace itself but not a trace of the headless man was found.

By this time some of the guests had left the palace thinking that the president was drunk or imagining things.

After a long search, the soldiers returned and reported to the chief guard that they had been unsuccessful.

'Sir,' one spoke with sad voice, 'we've searched everywhere but there was nothing to be seen.'

Then one of the guards spoke up that he was sure he had seen a body without a head or feet, but thought that he was drunk because when he looked again it wasn't there.

The Chief Guard knew that the President had given him an order that he must find the headless body and kill it or else he'd be jobless. He took a group of soldiers fully armed with him to the shallow grave.

They didn't know if the headless body had returned to his resting place or not, so they decided to uncover the grave and if the body was there make sure it was dead.

When they arrived at the grave they were afraid and dared not go near it. At length one brave solder said, 'I'll go but you'll have to promise me that if it suddenly pops up you'll shoot it quickly.'

'Sure,' they agreed. One soldier said, 'I'll shoot it quickly!'

While the brave soldier was approaching the grave the others got their guns ready to shoot at anything that moved.

Back at the palace, things couldn't have been tenser. The guests that had left must have spread the word that a man's headless body was rolling about in the palace. News travelled fast and crowds gathered quickly. The villagers had heard that a dead President had returned to the palace to take his revenge on those who had killed him.

Back at the shallow grave the group of soldiers had uncovered the grave, but there wasn't a trace of the body to be seen. Now the Chief Guard found himself in a spot. He dare not go back to the palace knowing that the body was still on the loose.

A few days passed and the headless body didn't come back to the palace and it was opened again to family and friends.

The President had regained some of his confidence but still felt insecure. At times he felt embarrassed for not fulfilling his official duties and wanted to be left alone, but was too scared to say goodbye to his guests. Some of his guests would dismiss themselves as they felt that something extraordinary was going on in the President's life, because they couldn't see the headless body. They thought it was all in his imagination.

The President began to believe that the headless body might have returned to its resting place and it was business as usual at the palace. Then one day the President received an invitation for himself and his family to be special guests at the world's richest car rally race.

The President's Chief Guard was one of the competitors and didn't believe that the old President's body would roll in again.

However he took a large group of guards along to the race just in case.

Now that he was among hundreds of excited people the President's family were excited, as this was their first public engagement since he had taken over as President. He was very glad to be out and about again. Now that he was among an excited crowd he had forgotten about his predecessor's threat that if any harm should come to him or his family he would see that the person or persons punished for their crimes.

It was a day at the races and the President and his family and those devoted to him were having a good day out. By this time spectators were all along the side of the racetrack for a closer view of the cars. The official circle was full of happy people and they were talking and drinking and telling jokes. The stadium was tightly guarded especially around the officials' circle where the President and his family were.

The race was less than 20 minutes old and the President's car was already in front of the others. It was being driven by the new Chief Guard; he was the people's favourite to win.

The President's car was very speedy and was in front from the start with the others strung out behind it. They were all hoping for a brilliant and exciting finish. The crowd was already full of excitement.

As the race progressed the cars began to spread out. There were only a few laps to go as the President's car began to pull clear of the others.

The President was thrilled to see his car heading towards the winning line and all the people who were sitting with him got out of their seats to celebrate when the car passed the winning post. The finishing line was just in front of the stadium and not far from the Presidential circle. Victory was assured as his Chief Guard pulled a long way clear of the others.

Then suddenly and unexpectedly, the headless body popped up again and began to roll past the officials' circle. But only the President had seen it and he was terrified. He urged his soldiers to open fire and insisted that they must not allow it to escape again. The soldiers got their guns ready but didn't fire because they couldn't see anything to shoot at. Those who had been seated near to the President thought that he was drunk again. When he grabbed one of the soldier's guns his guests began to run and take cover. The President opened fire at the headless body but only succeeded in shooting some of the spectators. Then, as he kept on shooting, the headless body rolled into the racetrack to intercept the President's car, which was a long way ahead of the others.

The driver was one of the five people who had murdered Bishop and when he was not far from the finishing line he looked in horror and saw a headless body rolling in front of him before the finishing line. The driver panicked and let go of the steering wheel and the car went out of control at full speed before smacking into an obstacle at the side of the track. Flames and smoke rose high into the sky as the headless President claimed his first victim.

Back at the stadium the crowds began to disperse and the soldiers took the President and his family back to his palace and placed armed guards around him. The situation got tenser now that the President's Chief Guard had died.

The person chosen to replace him would have to promise to find the headless body and kill it. This was the new agreement and they chose someone who was happy to take on the assignment.

The new Chief Guard began to lay out his plan to his guardsmen about how to make the headless body return to its place of rest. He told his men that the headless man had caused them to shoot at each other and that was ludicrous. He assembled another group of soldiers and interrogated the first group that had murdered the President. As they stood to attention, he began his speech by saying, 'We are convinced that the old President has come back with a vengeance and all those who are responsible for his death are going to be killed by him.'

They were all convinced that the Chief Guard who had died in the crash was just the first of his victims. The new Chief didn't have to put it into words as all those who had taken part began sweating, not knowing which of them would be next. The Chief Guard opened the meeting to suggestions about how they might help the President overcome his fears. One soldier came up with a brilliant suggestion, 'Chief, why don't you give an order to free the dead man's wife and family and then his body might stop rolling around and return to its place of rest?'

The Chief thought about it and said, 'We'll keep a close watch on the President's movements; if he starts shooting again we will console him and then release his family and friends.' What they didn't know at the time was that while the meeting was going on the headless body had made its way past them and into the palace where it remained unseen to everyone except the President. The headless man had a plan and he was determined to see it through. He had planned to show himself to the new President whenever he and the three guards who had killed him got together. Hopefully, the President might panic and shoot his own soldiers when trying to shoot his headless body.

Bishop had planned that all those who burned him to death would die – including the new President. Only then would he return to his place of rest. After the Chief Guard had brought the meeting to an end he posted armed guards in and around the President's quarters and said to him, 'Not even hell's terror will be able to pass us without being seen.'

After they had strengthened the guards around the President they waited and waited for the headless man but he didn't turn up. They thought that the headless man might have gone back to his rest and the new President was very glad. His new Chief had kept up the good work. Then one day the new President and the three men involved in the old President's death met together for a chat. It was time for the headless body to strike. Suddenly and unexpectedly the headless body popped up and started to roll in front of the President and close to his men. As soon as the new President saw the body rolling he shouted 'Guards, guards!' The three soldiers reached for their machine guns ready to shoot at anything that moved but they couldn't see anything to shoot at. This was the moment that the dead Bishop had been waiting for. All of the four people who killed him were tightly grouped including the new President. Bishop appeared before them! As the soldiers couldn't see Bishop headless body, the new President snatched a machine gun from one of his soldier and opened fire to try and kill the headless man but he shot three of the soldiers dead on the floor in front of him. The new Chief Guard heard the shooting got panicked and shot the new President dead. He fell to the floor between the other three soldiers that he'd killed.

The headless body had taken his revenge and now he had claimed the lives of the five people who had killed him and he went back into his shallow grave and remained there. The analysis of the headless man resulted in a revelation that, after the death of the real president, a foreign Government had sent some of their officers to investigate Bishop's death but seeing that they didn't have full authority of that island where the murder had taken place, the revelation showed them as headless bodies without hands or feet seeking to revenge Bishop Death.

Jeremy told Detective Doctor Whoot that he had tried to get to the President to warn him in time, but he had been assassinated before his very eyes.

Jeremy was there only as a witness to the crime and was locked in the palace where nobody was able to hear him. When Detective Whoot heard this he said, 'The authorities thought you might need some more help so we've sent some more officers to investigate the crime.

So you can be on the next plane home.'

Before Jeremy left the island he and two of the island's local officers went to check the computer records at the airport, with a slim hope that they could identify anyone fitting the description of the missing schoolgirl Gillian Walters or Tam from the Cruel Four Gang. Unfortunately there had been no one matching either description entering the country through the airport.

CHAPTER 18

THE FREEDOM FIGHTER

Back in South Africa, Michael went to his hotel that night but couldn't sleep and the next day he and Mick found themselves on the way to a new village where they arrived about dinnertime. Mick saw some very sad looking people and nudged Michael.

'What on earth has happened here? Let's ask that native woman over there,' he pointed.

She said that just before they came to the village a large, beautiful worm was born. It just suddenly popped out of the ground in the middle of a path. She pointed to the very spot where the worm had appeared.

Another lady described the worm to them. 'It has three stripes of different colours across its back. It's the most beautiful thing I've ever seen. I wish our country's flag were the same colours.

'So what has happened to the worm now?' Michael asked.

'It's been destroyed by soldiers from the cruel army,' she cried.

'Yes,' another lady declared, 'two soldiers came here and trampled on the worm until it was dead. Then they kicked it off the path and went on their way laughing.'

As she was talking, three baby worms suddenly appeared out of the dust – one of them had the same colours as the first. The natives were overwhelmed to see the new worms replace the first one. Word spread quickly and a large crowd of people gathered in the village. Some of them were soldiers from the nearby village.

They came to protect the worms from being killed again by the army. Michael and Mick were about to leave the village when they saw another soldier over six feet tall walk towards them with a limp. He had a holster round his hips, a rifle in his hand and a very mean looked on his face.

When Mick first saw him he gave Michael a nudge, 'If I'm not mistaken this soldier has come to put a solid defence around the new worms.'

CHAPTER 19

HUMANS CARCASSES IN THE FIELD

Now the scene had deepened. It was late night when Michael and Mick went back to the hotel. As soon as Michael rested his head upon his pillow and began to doze the night became day, the villagers began to protect the new worms from being killed and a fierce battle followed. There were many human carcasses lying on the ground being eaten by ravens.

After the violence ended the villages got together as one strong nation. Black and white people were working together for the good of their country and the fields were green again; the nation began to flourish. The trees had an abundance of fruits and the young deer returned to dine with their parents in a fruitful land. The days of war and depression were over and the natives' long dream for peace was finally accomplished. Michael looked up to the sky and saw writing on the cloud! It said that the land, which was once full of wickedness, was now of joy and peace.

'God, be praised,' said Michael. With a sigh of bewilderment, he bowed his head and prayed.

Then the verse of the scripture, Hosea 6, began to fill his imagination.

Two Chronicles Chapter 7: 13 said, 'If God shut up heavens that there is no rain, or if He commands the locusts to devour the land, or if He sends pestilence among His people'. But there is mercy with the Lord because verses 14 of the Scripture said, 'If my people, who are called by my name, shall humble themselves and pray, and seek God's face, and turn from their wicked ways then will God hear from heaven, and will forgive their sins, and will heal their land.' The writing was on the cloud.

CHAPTER 20

THE AEROBATIC SHOW

As the revelations deepened, early the next morning Michael and Mick found themselves at an aerodrome. It was quite an experience and there were many police officers there, as it was well guarded. Then it came to light that a young Prince and Princess were due to arrive at the air show in their private plane. After coming from a country of peace Michael had never seen anything like it before. As they stood there in amazement a helicopter arrived. To their surprise it was only the helicopter pilot and a passenger who was drunk.

One officer said to the other, 'See that he doesn't have any more champagne, as he might have to fly the helicopter back home'.

Then the man got out of the helicopter with two bottles of champagne and leant back on the helicopter with wobbly knees. He swayed backwards and forwards before falling to the ground. An officer went to help by taking him back inside the helicopter to sleep it off. The young Prince and Princess were late arriving so the aerobatic show was delayed. Everybody at the aerodrome was filled with excitement, waiting for the Prince and Princess to arrive. What they didn't know was that the President had been kidnapped and a false President was about to takes his place at the air show.

The crowd had settled down; the show was about to commence without the President because he had been delayed. The pilot, who was the people's favourite to win the show, had come from Great Britain.

Michael and Mick found themselves in the middle of a stadium full of excited people. The pilots had to follow a marked off route that was adventurous and highly dangerous with many tall trees in the way.

The pilots had very little space to manoeuvre their planes and as the day wore on the tension grew with all eyes on the British pilot. Then suddenly and unexpectedly the British pilot pulled off one of the biggest tricks that caused the crowd to hold their breath. The pilot took his plane high up in the sky then twisted and turned before flying low and disappearing behind the tall trees.

The crowd couldn't see the plane at that point but heard when it hit the ground and core of the earth with one of its wings. They all thought the plane had crashed but were amazed when the pilot came into view. The noise was thunderous as the crowd cheered and clapped. They never thought that the pilot had made it back into the sky! His performance was absolutely fantastic. Then while Michael and Mick were standing in the crowd of happy people Michael caught sight of a man he had seen in England not many days before he went to South Africa. He gave Mick a nudge, 'This is a small world. I've just seen a man I saw in England before I came here.'

'Well,' Mick said, 'let's go and have a chat with him.'

Just before they got there the man lost them in the crowd. The crowds were still waiting for the planes to appear out of the cloudy sky when they heard that the President had delayed his arrival. Michael and Mick went through the crowd and came upon a young native boy. The boy approached with a broken red guitar in his hand, 'Please mister,' he said, 'can either of you fix this guitar for me?' Mick immediately looked at Michael and the boy handed him 36 small nails. 'I'm not a musician!' Mick said to the boy, 'and this isn't the place for us to fix anything.'

'I know that,' the boy replied and pointed to a large building on the other side of the road surrounded by stone walls. 'There's the workshop,' he spoke joyfully. Michael and Mick and the young native boy climbed over the wall and ended up in a cemetery that was at the back of the large building. The workshop was at the front.

As they were walking through the cemetery towards the front of the building they heard some people talking as if they were having an argument. Michael and Mick were afraid of who those people might be, as they thought that the police were there to make an arrest. They decided to creep up quietly and have a closer look to see what the fuss was all about. When they got close they saw the group of men who had kidnapped the young President from his plane. The President couldn't resist, as there were too many of them.

'This is a kidnapping case,' Michael said to the others. 'Let's creep up a little closer and see what they are going to do with the President.'

So Michael, Mick and the young native boy got nearer to the building and hid there to watch.

The group of armed men stripped the President of his clothes and dressed him in different clothing. One of them pushed him, 'Sit down in the chair!' Then they tied his hand and feet.

Within the space of five minutes a large articulated lorry came into the building with the President's plane strapped down on the truck. Then the group of armed men lifted the President and put him into the truck and drove away.

'My, my,' Michael breathed out, astonished that they had just witnessed a kidnapping.

They could have panicked.

'Mick,' said Michael 'I'm out of here and you better come with me!' They left the young native boy to go back to the stadium to raise the alarm and went to the immigration records office to find out if any of the Cruel Four gang had come to South Africa to hide from the police.

CHAPTER 21

TWIN MOON ISLAND

After he described the suspect they didn't have any record of such a person's arrival in the country at that time or date. Michael left the record office and headed for home.

Mick remained in South Africa because Michael told him that he would ask Detective Doctor David Whoot for help in freeing his son from the South African jail. Then he made his way to the airport to catch a flight back to Great Britain.

After Detective Michael Felix and Jeremy Ashman had returned from their assignments they went to the office to see Detective Doctor Whoot. Michael was the first to give details of his investigations in South Africa. Michael told them of the stranger he had met on his way towards the aerobatic show where he saw the young President kidnapped.

As soon as Michael said this Jeremy said, 'Well, that story sounds just like a dream I had.'

One officer looked at Jeremy, 'Did you say you had a dream?'

"Yes,' Jeremy said, 'I had a dream, what's wrong with that?'

They all looked at Jeremy with a smile saying, 'We just can't wait to hear what your dream was about!'

'Well,' Jeremy spoke, 'I have a gift that helps me to dream up things to come. They might come to pass now or they may take many years. We'll just have to wait and see.' Then Jeremy looked at them, 'The dream I had was of fear and excitement.'

'We can't wait to hear it,' said one officer.

The other said, 'Bring it on.'

Then Jeremy began looking back to 1 July 1980 when he lived with his aunt Kerry Henry. He was in bed tucked up under what he thought to be his duvet cover, feeling warm and cosy before he went off to sleep.

While he snoozed his Aunt and her younger niece, Lee, came into his room in a panic.

'Jeremy' they said, frightened, 'wake up, and wake up.'

Jeremy was feeling so warm in bed he didn't want to be disturbed.

'Lee,' he spoke softly, 'go away and get back to your bed!'

After he said this he turned from one side to the other without opening his eyes.

Lee shook him again, 'Jeremy you better wake up, you're not at home in bed as you might suppose.'

'So, where am I then?' he asked without moving the duvet covering his head.

Lee shook him again saying, 'if you really want to know where you are why don't you open your eyes and look!'

As he was somewhat doubtful, Lee said, 'Ok, let me tell you. We're in a bush land and you're lying beneath a tree with your head rested on the root of the tree and your hands as pillows behind your head.'

As soon as Lee said this Jeremy leaped up and opened his eyes. You should have seen the look of surprise appear on his face. He was indeed bewildered. He turned with frightened eyes and saw the dense woodland around them. He was dumbfounded. Neither he nor Lee knew how this had happened or where in the world they were. They looked at each other with astonishment because this was an unexplainable situation.

They found themselves on an island that nobody else had visited before and they were amazed.

The island looked as if it had been forgotten for several generations, yet it was full of young trees and low undergrowth. Jeremy couldn't believe his eyes as he looked all around.

'Lee,' he spoke quietly, 'where in the world are we? Which way is the way home?'

There wasn't an answer to this unexplainable mystery that filled their hearts with astonishment and despair. They stood for a moment and looked towards the distance but there wasn't a district to be seen. All that they saw were fields of trees, mountains of great rocks looming up and a deep valley below and many beautiful landscapes in the distance.

The adventurous land had a mixture of drama in paradise. Then Lee looked at Jeremy, 'Does this place look familiar – as if we've been here before?' How wrong was Lee? As a matter of fact Lee was very wrong. Twin moons have two brand new islands upon them and unbeknown to Jeremy and Lee they had discovered the first island.

As they walked on they came to a high mountain in the way that they had to climb. The valley below was breathtaking. They couldn't think of which way to go – not to the north, or to the south, or to the west, or to the east. Which way would take them back home?

'Lee,' Jeremy said, 'let's climb up the side of the high mountain and see what's on the other side of the mountain.' As soon as they got up the side of the mountain they started to shout with all the loudness of their voices, 'Hello is any one there? Can anyone hear us?'

They shouted this way once or twice but got no reply. Poor souls, they were not aware that from the very minute they arrived upon Twin Moon Island a gigantic creature was aware of them coming. It immediately started to make tracks to find the visitors and kill them.

As it seemed the marauder had a thirst for human blood.

Jeremy and Lee should have thanked their lucky stars that the stalker was several days away from catching up with them.

After they had shouted and got no reply Lee looked at Jeremy. 'What are we going to do now? Where are we heading to?'

This she asked through her tears and a little sweat appeared on her forehead and her face began to sweat. Jeremy looked at Lee and saw that she was scared to death of been lost.

'Oh, I see,' Jeremy uttered, 'you're now crying like a little baby: I can't believe it.'

Jeremy said this but he was just trying to be brave so that his cousin might take hope and courage.

They set off again, walking with a hope that they might find a place to rest before nightfall. Jeremy thought that if they kept walking they might come upon a road that leads to somewhere.

They went on walking, with not the least idea of where they were heading to, or what they might encounter on the way. They now reached the edge of a mountain.

'Lee,' Jeremy uttered, 'let's try and climb to the top of that mountain over there. We might have a clearer view of what's on the other side of the mountain.'

What they saw was a beautiful landscape on the other side of the deep valley but there wasn't a building in sight.

'Lee,' Jeremy said. 'I tell you what! We'll use the mountains over there as a landmark and mark out a trail with our eyes and follow that trail. If we are lost we will return to the mountain and start again.'

To reach the landscape on the other side of the valley was a very difficult trail with creeping weeds and thick undergrowth that was tangled in the way. Was the way to the valley more than they were able to cope with? After some hours of struggling they came to an open area from where they had a clear view of the landscape across the valley.

'What a beautiful place,' said Lee.

There were hills above hills until the sky became level with the hills. By this time the evening was fast approaching. They had made every effort to get through the valley before it got dark. The calmness on the beautiful island caused the visitors to become puzzled. They came to realise that there weren't any sights or sounds of woodland creatures. They stood for a moment to listen. They were right; as a matter of fact there wasn't even the distant hooting of an owl to be heard.

Before they continued any further Jeremy looked around, 'This island has formed a picture in my mind'.

Lee spoke hastily with a giggle and said, 'a picture what kind of a picture would that be?'

Jeremy replied, 'This place looks more like a place where people would visit in their dreams.'

Lee looked at him and laughed. 'This place looks real enough to me.' As soon as he said this he paused and a trickle of tears fell from his eyes. Jeremy knew they might be in quite a dangerous situation and Lee was only 12 years old. Being the oldest he had to act as if everything was alright, but deep down in his heart he was terrified of becoming lost. Then he looked at Lee crying.

'Lee, let's just say for an instant that we are lost. After all, to be lost away from home and end up on a beautiful island like this, what's the use of worrying? After all, people get lost at some time or another and have to make the best of the situation until they either find their way home or get rescued by someone.'

Poor Jeremy couldn't tell where his gift would lead them to.

Then Lee spoke up again, 'Jeremy what if when we got over the valley nobody lives there? What are we going to do then?'

Jeremy kept his mouth firmly shut and went on walking.

By this time the day had almost gone and the shadows of dark were creeping up into the valley. As they were heading towards the bottom of the hill, Lee cried out, 'I'm exhausted. Jeremy, please, my leg is hurting. Can't we just stop here for a moment to rest?'

'Oh no,' Jeremy disagreed. 'We'll carry on and try to make it across the valley before it gets dark.'

'Ok then,' Lee agreed.

Then Jeremy looked across the valley to the hill and caught sight of a yellow sandy area that looked like an old riverbed. Then the most amazing thing happened. Before they reached the middle of the valley they came across many fruit trees, some of which were loaded with green and ripe fruits! This was quite an unusual scene as all the other trees on the island weren't old enough to bear fruits. As soon as Lee saw the fruit trees she immediately regained strength and got excited.

'Let's see who will get to the fruit trees first.' Despite being hungry Jeremy didn't know if the fruits were safe to eat.

'Lee,' he shouted out loud, 'please don't eat any of the fruits until I get there! Did you hear me?'

'Yes,' she replied, 'hurry up then!'

When Jeremy got there he saw Lee stood beneath one of the fruit tree anxiously waiting to taste the fruits.

By this time the creature was a long way from catching up to them.

As soon as Jeremy got to the fruit trees he picked one of the fruits from off the ground. There were many on the ground as well as on the trees! He took some time and examined the fruit closely.

'They are very beautiful, aren't they?' and threw one in the air like a ball.

Wow!' uttered Lee. Then the big question arrived. How were they going to know if the fruit was safe enough to eat?

Jeremy decided that being the oldest he should eat the fruit first. Lee got scared said, 'Oh, no, I'll eat first because if the fruit should make you ill, what would I do then without you?'

As soon as she said this Jeremy timidly put one of the fruit to his mouth and took a large bite of it and chewed it for a minute or so and swallowed it. 'Wow,' he gasped out astonished, it's gorgeous!'

Then he took a much bigger bite of the fruit and then another. After that they stood in silence, waiting to see what effect the fruit would have on Jeremy. Lee kept watchful eyes on Jeremy hoping that he'd be alright. Every so often she asked Jeremy, 'how do you feel now?'

'So far, so good!' he replied. Then after they had waited for about 20 minutes Lee asked if it was alright for her to eat the fruit.

Jeremy said, 'You can wait a little longer.'

CHAPTER 22

A MOONLESS NIGHT

But after they'd waited for another 20 minutes or so nothing was wrong with Jeremy so they both ate a bellyful of the fruit and took some with them for their journey in the morning. Jeremy stood on the top of the hill and looked down into the valley; soon it would be getting dark. He knew perfectly well that they'd have to find a safe place to rest for the night.

Jeremy went above the valley and walked along the edge of the hill until he came upon a place that was less scary than the others.

Lee looked at him and said, 'Do you mean that we are going to sleep here at the edge of the valley all night?'

'Sure, he replied, what's wrong with that? As you can see there isn't a safer place than this. But don't worry; I think we'll be alright here.'

Lee agreed and they went off to gather some sticks, twigs and tree limbs to make themselves a little hut.

Young Lee was very afraid of the dark. Jeremy allowed her to have the first sleep while he kept watch. Jeremy put some dry bushes around the hut as an alarm if any prowlers should attack while they were asleep.

Lee went in first and lay down to rest but being afraid of the dark woodland she couldn't sleep. As the woodland grew darker and darker she turned from one side to the other.

'Jeremy,' she mumbled. 'I can't sleep; can you try and make up a story?'

'Very well,' Jeremy said, 'I'll try and think of a story that is so boring you'll surely goes off to sleep.'

'Ha, ha, ha!' Lee laughed. 'Try me,' she said with a smile.

Jeremy knew quite well that Lee was too scared to go to sleep.

He begins the story by saying; Poor Katrina Stanford had lived alone in the country. Her farm house had no electricity. So at night she had her fireplace full of burning logs.

She had work all day and sleep all night. At length she was pretty bored; because she didn't have a television nor anybody to talk to.

Then one evening before she went to bed she looked up and saw a cloudless sky.

She thought it was going to be a moonlit night so she planned to have a picnic among the animals!'

She put her picnic basket beside her and sat waiting for the moon to shine. In her error the night grew darker and darker.

'What has happen to the moon?' she wondered.

She didn't know this but the guy who lives on the moon went out early that morning for a stroll. Returning again walking he began to struggled with a large bundle of wood on his back. Walking slowly he didn't reach home in time to make up the fire that lit up the moon. So the earth didn't have any moonlight that night.

As soon as Jeremy got this far...

'Wow,' Lee gasped, astonished.

'Jeremy' Lee spoke excitedly – that was some story. Do you think story about the man who lived on the moon is true? Do you?'

'Come on, Lee,' uttered Jeremy, 'are you having a laugh? If you're thinking that we are on that moon, how could we have got to the moon? Did we come here by flight?'

'Oh no, we had, not.

'You do agree that we haven't got any wings, don't you?

However if the story that you heard about the man on the moon is true, then hopefully we might meet him one day. Then we could be a very famous moon characters! Just think about it.'

As soon as Jeremy said this, Lee got scared and covered up her face with her hands saying, 'I wish it was daylight.'

Jeremy looked at her. He knew quite well that Lee had spoken cowardly, so Jeremy kept his mouth firmly shut and leaned back to rest.

Had Jeremy and his cousin Lee know they had been threatened by a marauder they would have surely panicked. The beast that is tracking them was getting closer.

Next day Jeremy and Lee found themselves walking towards the south of the island. They had taken the higher ground to avoid going through the dense part of the valley. They kept a certain landscape as a landmark in case they had to turn back the way they came. After they'd travelled 20 miles through ragged ground Lee looked towards the distance and saw a large stretch of yellow sand.

As soon as Lee saw this she got excited. 'Jeremy,' she shouted out loud and excitedly, 'let's sees who can get their first!'

Before Jeremy could reply Lee went running off like a frisky unicorn without looking back to see if Jeremy was following.

Jeremy shouted, 'Lee, stop and wait for me'.

But Lee didn't seem to hear a word and Jeremy ran after him but being the youngest Jeremy who barely had enough breath to catch up with her. Lee ran on until she was out of sight. Jeremy didn't know that the ravenous beast was on their tail and wasn't too far away so the worst was yet to come. Jeremy went running after Lee until he was breathless. At length he reached the yellow-sanded area but Lee wasn't there. His heart dropped as Lee should have been waiting for him.

'Oh, my God,' Jeremy breathed out, 'where could she have gone to?'

With a worried mind he turned and looked around the stretch of yellow sand that was like an old dried up riverbed full of trees, sand and weeds. But Lee was nowhere to be seen.

Jeremy knew the island was a very remote place. If anything had happened there would be no one there to help. Jeremy took another look around but there wasn't any sign of Lee.

He climbed to the top of a mountain and looked for any movement among the trees. He turned his face towards the valley and shouted out loud, 'Lee, can you hear me?' He stopped to listen but only heard the echo of his own voice.

Then he heard some loose stones falling from the hill towards the valley. 'Lee,' he shouted softly, 'are you there?'

There was no reply so he went to the very spot where the loose stones had rolled from but there wasn't any sign of Lee.

He began thinking that Lee had taken too much fancy to the strange island and knew not where the danger lay. By this time the day had got much older and the sun had risen to spread bright light over the valley and the beautiful landscapes on the other side of the valley.

As he was climbing down the hill with his mind full of uncertainty he heard the sound of a gigantic creature roar with loudness in its voice, as if it was ready to kill anything in its way.

Poor Jeremy had no clear direction of where the creature might be coming from. The sound of the creature's voice echoed everywhere over the valley. Jeremy thought of Lee and his mind went in to a complete jumble. 'Oh, my God,' he cried out fearfully.

He knew quite well that Lee would be frightened out of her wits. Jeremy began to pray, asking for the Lord God to help him find Lee quickly before the beast got hold of her.

CHAPTER 23

THE STEGOSAURUS

As he was running and sliding down the hill towards the valley he caught sight of Lee walking backwards. King Stegosaurus at this time was only a short distance away.

'Oh, my God, this is it!' Jeremy cried. Lee must have seen the creature and was too afraid to turn her back on it. To add more to the terror, Jeremy saw a long precipice not far from where Lee was walking.

Jeremy was a distance away from catching up to Lee. 'Lee, stop! Turn around. Look where you are going: there's a precipice behind you – please stop.'

But Lee didn't turn to look at Jeremy and just kept walking backwards. Jeremy knew quite well that if Lee didn't stop or turn round she would fall into the precipice.

The creature began yelling again and the echoes of its voice sounded everywhere over the valley. This caused Lee to panic even more. It now seemed that Lee had gone completely deaf and dumb and instead of slowing her stride she quickened it.

Jeremy was still a distance away and threw himself flat to the ground and reached out with both hands but wasn't near enough. Lee went flying backwards towards the precipice.

'Oh my God,' Jeremy uttered. He was dumfounded and lay on the edge of the cliff, frozen stiff.

As soon as he had regained his sanity he took a timid look at the rock face with tears in his eyes. It was as if Lee had fallen over the edge of the world.

Then worst of all, he didn't know which direction the creature would appear from. With trembling knees he took another peep over the cliff face. He couldn't face up to the fact that Lee had fallen over the precipice and was now alone. She might have hurt herself and was lying somewhere that nobody could help her.

With eyes full of tears Jeremy called unto the Lord again and asked for His help. Then suddenly the mystery deepened. Jeremy stood on the edge of the cliff and shouted, 'Lee if you can hear me please reply.'

Then he looked and saw the creature at a distance running at full speed towards the cliff over which Lee had fallen. Jeremy looked over the cliff again and caught sight of something that looked like a person sat crouching down with her head on her knees.

He thought that it was Lee. He said, 'Thank you Lord for hearing my prayer.'

'Lee, he shouted are you there, are you hurt?'

He listened to a faint cry coming from below saying, 'Jeremy I'm here on the new moon surface!'

Jeremy thought that Lee might have knocked his head and was having a delusion.

'Lee, can you hear me?'

'Yes.'

'Lee if you are able to walk please gets into an open place where I can see you!'

'Sure,' she replied faintly. Then she went to an open spot and lifted up a hand saying. 'Jeremy I'm here!'

As soon as Jeremy saw Lee, he lifted up his head and looked toward the heavens. 'Thank you Lord!'

He knew quite well that it was God who had performed this miracle because the first time he had looked over the cliff it seemed like a bottomless pit.

Now that he was able to see Lee clearly he began to act quickly. At this point the creature was heading directly towards young Lee, but Jeremy did not tell her as she might panic some more.

'Lee,' Jeremy shouted, 'are you sure you're okay?'

'Yes,' she said, 'I'm okay but hurry up, I'm scared!'

'Just hang on, I won't be long now.'

He could see the creature more clearly now – it was brown and about six foot. It was moving with all its force, parting the young trees in its way. The beast was only a short distance away from where they were.

Jeremy went back to the edge of the cliff. 'Lee,' he shouted, 'do you think you'll able to climb into one of those trees over there?' and pointed.

Lee went to the slender tree that wasn't far from the wall of precipice.

I'll try,' she said.

'I want you to try and climb up the tree and if the creature should yell again please do not panic just hold on tightly.'

The plan that Jeremy had to rescue Lee was highly adventurous and very dangerous. Should it fail then both of them would fall to the destruction of the creature.

Now it was time to rescue Lee. Jeremy went back to the edge of the cliff to give Lee the final instructions.

'Lee,' he shouted, 'please does not panic, I have made a plan and between you and me we can make it work! This is what I want you to do; whenever I shout your name start to sway the tree. By shifting your weight back and forth and when the tree is in full swing and close to me, stretch out one of your hands and I'll pull you from the tree.'

As soon as he gave Lee the instructions the creature appeared beneath the tree and started to act as if it was a human being. And a king of the place that Lee called the new moon surface.

As far as the King Stegosaurus was concerned, Lee and Jeremy were unwelcome guests. It was very angry. It galloped here and there in a circle beneath the tree, slamming its tail into the ground in protest. Then it began making a grunting noise as to say, 'Get off my territory or else the worst is yet to come.'

Jeremy stood for a moment looking at the creature and couldn't believe his eyes at its behaviour. It was huge and angry. After it had stamped its authority on the area it came back beneath the tree Lee was on. Jeremy began to act quickly and bent down one of the young trees and stretched it with all his strength.

Then he shouted at Lee to begin swinging on the tree. This was a life or death situation. Lee swung the tree until it was close to Jeremy who reached out with one of his hands but missed Lee's hand and grabbed a tree branch instead. Then the tree swung back and Jeremy went flying over the edge of the cliff and landed flat on his back to lay helplessly on the new moon surface.

As sooner as the stegosaurus heard Jeremy land on the ground it immediately left the tree and went to get Jeremy. When Lee looked and saw the bloodthirsty beast going towards Jeremy she climbed down from the tree and provoked the stegosaurus to turn away from Jeremy. Lee dodged the beast and went quickly to help Jeremy off the ground.

Then they saw the gigantic creature ploughing through the young trees, coming towards them with great force. They were terrified and didn't have anywhere to escape and they were not far from the edge of another cliff.

Then in a terrifying moment another miracle happened; suddenly they saw the creature's head pull back and it came to a sudden stop.

Jeremy looked at Lee with tears of joy. 'Something has got hold of the stegosaurus!' They thought it had been caught by creeping weeds that were tangled in the way, but it was strangled by a chain around its neck and tied to a tree! Who had done this, they wondered.

Lee stood a short distance away from the creature because it was very angry.

CHAPTER 24

THE MOVING PLANET

Jeremy looked up to the sky, 'Thank you Lord!' he prayed.

Then it became known to him by a revelation that he and Lee has fallen from one new moon to the other. They were bewildered.

One of the moons was at the top, the other at the bottom. The amazing thing was that whenever one of the moons moved, the other would follow yet they weren't attached to each other!

As they were standing there amazed they saw King Stegosaurus trying with its utmost power to break loose from its chain.

'Lee,' Jeremy shouted, 'we'll have to run!'

They then hear a sound like an earthquake and the earth began to shake. The planets began moving – one above and one below. They were like twin sisters – anywhere one went, the other followed.

Jeremy and Lee kept on running while the two great islands kept moving. Which way the moons were heading wasn't clear. After they had run about five miles through wild terrain they came to a mountain and sat there to rest. Lee was so tired she just slung herself down to the ground, gasping for breath.

'Well,' Jeremy said, 'we've come a long way. If the creature breaks loose now we have a good start ahead of it. I was just thinking that dinosaurs might have roamed the earth below some thousands of years ago. They would be surprised to know that the king of the creatures is still alive today and has made the Twin Moons Island his home.'

Then Lee became scared saying, 'What if one of them should just suddenly attack us? Where would we go?'

'Lee,' Jeremy uttered, 'you're always thinking of the worst, aren't you?'

Then they went to find a safe place to rest for the night and to continue their journey in the morning.

Next day Jeremy woke up to a new situation and found himself alone and walking on a travelling moon. The moons went from stage to stage but Jeremy kept walking, not knowing where he was going. He walked and came to a beautiful patch, which was most adventurous. There were many acres of well-kept turf like a massive golf course.

'Right,' Jeremy said to him, 'I'll take a rest here'.

At the very moment he sat to rest, the twin moons suddenly separated themselves from each other. The one on which Jeremy was travelling suddenly went down to rest upon a great sea and joined land to land with another island.

CHAPTER 25

THE MOON CAME TO REST UPON THE SEA

The transformation of the moon happened in the nick of time. As quick as Jeremy could blink an eyelid there was no more sea. As he was standing there alone and amazed at the wonders of the Lord God, he took a distant look and saw the wreckage of a ship laying on the sandy beach with two tall flag masts flapping in the wind.

As soon as he saw the wreckage of the ship he thought that home couldn't be too far away.

Jeremy was on his way towards the wrecked ship when he caught sight of a young boy who was probably the same age as his cousin Lee – about 12 years old.

The boy came running from the old island and with a leap he landed on the new Moon Island, which was partly in flame at the time.

As soon as Jeremy saw the boy he was anxious to know where he had come from and where he was going. To avoid an accident he reached out to rescue the boy who was headed straight into a danger area. At this time some parts of the new surface were heaving with electricity and sparking heavily.

While Jeremy was running after the boy he was trying to make his presence less scary, so that the boy might not think he was going to harm him. As the chase progressed Jeremy came upon an area of the surface that had several blocks of iron pipes lying on the ground, some of which were sparkling although they weren't grounded.

As this was in a remote area and if there was an emergency he wouldn't have any help if he decided to stop the boy from jumping from one block of iron piping to the other so he wouldn't get an electricity shock.

The question Jeremy had in mind was this, 'what has caused a 12-year-old boy to play upon a dangerous moon surface?'

'Young man,' he shouted, 'please does not jump from one of those iron pipes to the other.'

'Why?' he asked grumpily and then ignored Jeremy's instruction and jumped again.

As soon as he jumped he lost his balance and fell backwards.
'Are you hurt?' Jeremy asked the boy because he was crying.
'I've injured my back,' he said.
So Jeremy went and tidied up his bruised knees, but he would not tell Jeremy his name or where he had come from.
Jeremy saw that he was about to run off again.
'Young man, you haven't given me your name or where you live. Is your home far from here?'
The boy just blanked him and continued running.
By this time the day had grown much older and the heat was great. Jeremy couldn't tolerate it any longer, but didn't want to leave the boy alone in the dangerous area.

Than the boy suddenly ran in another direction at top speed and left him far behind running on at a slower speed. He struggled until he came upon a new area, which was like paradise compared to the others they had passed through. This place was a beautiful place, the air was fresh and the trees were very green. It was now early morning, the sun had risen and the day was getting brighter.

CHAPTER 26

THE MOON CHARACTERS

Jeremy looked towards the distance and caught sight of the boy running further in the new direction.

'Young man,' he shouted, 'what are you running away from? If it's me, I'm only trying to help, but you won't stop and talk to me!'

The boy didn't reply or stop but just kept running.

'Well,' Jeremy shouted, 'you're just a horrible creature!'

As soon as Jeremy said this, he heard a man's voice from a distance away, 'Mr, couldn't you find a better name to call the boy than a horrible creature?'

At long last, Jeremy spoke, astonished. He had finally come to an area where people lived. He was filled with joy and so excited he told the stranger why he had called the boy that name. All he wanted was to know if the boy had lost his way as he himself felt lost.

As he was standing there, an aeroplane flew low over them. At the same time a middle-aged man and a beautiful young woman came to talk to him. The gentleman gave Jeremy his hand and the young lady told him that she was an actress and pointed to a camera and equipment that lay on the ground. As he was talking with the young lady another plane flew low and dropped two bombs near the beautiful actress.

'Wow,' Jeremy gasped astonished, he thought someone had meant to harm her but she explained that it was a part of an act.

While they were laughing a young man flew over in a glider that was shaped like an aeroplane.

'Hello,' Jeremy shouted to the young man in the glider, 'can you see a young boy from up there?'

He pointed in the direction the boy had gone.

'I've seen him,' the young man said, 'he's gone to see the preacher.'

'A preacher,' Jeremy spoke excitedly, 'how far away is that?'

The actress said that she wouldn't advise Jeremy to go after the boy because he might not find the way back.

Then the vision ended. They all gave Jeremy a clap and one officer said that Jeremy should write a book about his story.

Three months later Jeremy and his family went to the office of Detective Sergeant Keen. Detective Doctor David Whoot was also there. They took Jeremy and his family and Buddy the sparrow to one of their activities. Jeremy and his family had an unforgettable day out and when the visit was over he and his family were about to leave Sally thanked the detectives for giving them such a remarkable time. The Detectives said goodbye to them and nothing else was said as they made their way home.

CHAPTER 27

LINDA'S HOUSE PARTY

Not long after Jeremy and his family had returned from visiting Detective Whoot, one Saturday morning while he and his wife was in bed the postman came and a letter was delivered. Sally got out of bed and went downstairs. It was an invitation for her and Jeremy. She took the letter and went back upstairs to read it to him.

As soon as she went into the bedroom she said, 'Jeremy guesses what! Linda and Dave have invited us to their house warming party.'

'Wow!' Jeremy breathed out, 'when is the happy day?'

She looked at the letter again. The party was in two weeks' time at Linda's new house in the beautiful Yorkshire Dales.

Sally and Jeremy didn't know this, but they were the first guests to be invited by Linda and Dave, who had been friends from school days.

Sally thought for a moment and said, 'Jeremy dear, I was just thinking, where I am going to get a trustworthy babysitter?'

Jeremy looked at her with a smile, 'Sally, don't you think it's a bit early to be thinking about babysitters?'

'Well,' she mumbled, we'll talk about this later.'

Then she went downstairs to do her domestic duties.

Sally couldn't wait for the day of the party to come. Visiting the Dales was just like having a holiday abroad compared to where they lived.

Later that day when they had gone to bed they heard two people talking outside their window. Jeremy got up and parted the curtains to look outside. He saw two men wearing hooded coats talking. One was slimly built and the other was plump and medium height. As he was looking, one of the neighbour's cats came purring and rubbing itself against one of the men's feet.

He looked down at the cat with a grumpy expression on his face before stepping back a few strides and kicking the cat it as if it was a rugby ball. The poor cat went flying through the air and landed in another neighbour's garden. The men looked at each other and laughed.

Jeremy wanted to shout at them, but knowing that the world is full of cowards ready to use a knife and gun even on the most fragile of people he kept his mouth firmly closed and wondered where humanity had gone to.

Within the space of ten minutes he looked again and the two men were still there.

Sally said, 'Let's call the police', but when she picked up the telephone it was dead.

'Jeremy!' She thought that the guys might have cut the telephone line that lead to the house, he looked outside again but as nobody was there they went back to bed.

CHAPTER 28

THE CROWN JEWELS

When they went to bed the next night Jeremy, who has the unusual gift of prophetic visions began to dream. The night became day and he and his family found themselves seated in their living room. The children were watching television. Then suddenly they heard the sound of an ambulance siren and the fire brigade going in the same direction.

'Wait a minute,' Jeremy said to his wife, 'have you heard that?'

'Yes,' she said, 'there must be an emergency somewhere.'

Then immediately a news flash came on the television about a train crash on the other side of the city that morning. The news showed the scene of the crash that wasn't far from where Jeremy and his family lived.

They were asking for volunteer to help and as soon as heard this he gave his wife a kiss saying, 'Darling I'll see you later.'

He went through the door and started driving towards the sound of the police sirens. At length he found himself on a road bridge with a river beneath it. The train crash was on the other side of the bridge. There were many emergencies vehicles and a lot of dead and injured people being helped by local volunteers who were working to free those who were trapped in the train. Jeremy heard a soft-spoken voice speak up and said, 'I've brought good news.'

He looked around quickly to see who it was and a little bird said, 'It is I who has brought the good news.'

'My goodness,' Jeremy uttered with surprise. He thought that, even in the worst of situations, there was excitement as the bird flew round and round him.

'Well, little bird, what good news could you have brought at a time like this?'

The bird answered, 'I've just heard that the lady of authority that was on the train this morning had not died!'

All those who heard the bird say this were overwhelmed with joy to know that the lady had not died.

Then the bird spoke up again, 'The lady of authority has not died, but thieves have stolen her crown jewels.'

'Good gracious,' uttered one stranger and another said that they were sad to hear of the lady's misfortune but glad that she was still alive. 'How could anyone steal at an accident like this? It is a disgusting type of person who doesn't have any human feelings, only greed.'

After the little bird had flown away it seemed that an opportunity had arrived for the thieves with the crown jewels to make their getaway. The police were busy helping at the crash and didn't even know that a robbery had been committed on the train.

The thieves were about to make their getaway and take Jeremy and some of the other workers hostage. One of the thieves told those they had kidnapped that he had a gun and if they refused to go with them he would use it.

They took the kidnapped people to an outcrop of land in the countryside. There were old loading bays not far from the country road.

The police by this time must have discovered the robbery as police car sirens could be heard going up and down the road, which was near the thieves' hideout. But they hid themselves in silence and waited until the police cars had gone. Then one of the thieves shouted to another, 'I want someone to go to the shop.' He said this while pointing his gun at those they had kidnapped.

One of the thieves gave a warning, 'We know the police are looking for us,' whilst pointing the gun at them.

He said to one of the kidnapped that they would be going to the shop for them. They knew that the thieves were only waiting for an opportunity to make their final getaway but now they were getting very angry and were afraid to show their faces at the shop.

They whispered privately amongst themselves that one of them should follow the guy who was going to the shop to keep an eye on him. There was a little country shop down the road, not far away from the old loading bays. One of the thieves gave each of the hostages twelve and a half-pence in the old currency of pounds, shillings and pence and told them to buy something to eat.

He pointed his gun at the one going to the shop, 'If you know what's best for you you'll keep your mouth shut about telling the police about us. If you get to the main road and you see the police you better not say anything to them or else your friends get this.' He clicked his gun.

After they had gone to the shop the main thief became worried and restless. 'What was I thinking? I've forgotten to order a bottle of whisky.'

He thought of sending someone else, but as there were only three of them he changed his mind.

However the same guy approached the hostages and said, 'I shall set you free when the time comes.'

After he said this one of the hostages whispered to another, 'Let's all pray that he keeps his promise and sets us free.'

It was now approaching the evening and the thieves were getting ready to go. Then the hostages saw the thieves' truck creeping slowly away.

'Yes,' one of them shouted out gladly. 'It seems that they have kept their promise and now we are free.'

As soon as the thieves were gone and they were on their way home it started to snow.

Before Jeremy got home he reported the kidnappers to the detectives and they promised to investigate the crime. By the time Jeremy got home the snow was so thick on the ground it seemed that it had been falling all day.

CHAPTER 29

A TALKING SPARROW

While Jeremy was inside his house looking out through the living room window at his children playing in the snow and his thoughts went back to the day he met Buddy, the talking sparrow. It was in February 1978 suddenly and unexpectedly he found himself outside standing in his back garden, which was covered with snow. Suddenly a sparrow came to rest upon a rose branch nearby.

Jeremy was quite excited to see the sparrow come so near to him.

Suddenly the sparrow began talking, Jeremy was absolutely dumbstruck. He had heard of a talking parrots but he'd never heard of talking sparrows before!

After a few days Jeremy and the sparrow built up a close relationship. He loved the bird and named it, Buddy. It was a very special sparrow with the unusual gift of being able to predict incoming danger. Then one day the worst came to light. Buddy had detected that a nuclear accident was about to happen.

When Jeremy heard this he cried out fearfully, 'Buddy, do you know whereabouts in the world this nuclear accident is going to take place?'

'Yes,' the sparrow declared. 'Somewhere in Europe – there are six nuclear missiles buried underground. For several years now they have not been maintained and Buddy thinks that they are in danger of exploding.'

'Oh, my God,' Jeremy uttered. Then, to add more to his fear, the sparrow said that the missiles had been programmed to fly to neighbouring countries, including Britain where thousands of people could die. So Jeremy decided to write about the sparrow's story, as it might be an early warning.

By this time the sparrow had become close friends with Jeremy who told Detective Doctor Whoot of the sparrow's special abilities and he made the bird an offer to work with Jeremy. They didn't know how the sparrow was able to talk in English, yet the fact remained that it was able to do so.

Jeremy was very proud to have a talking sparrow, as it was telling him the stories he should write about. He began to depend on Buddy and Buddy depended on him to pass on his messages. The bird knew perfectly well that some of the stories might carry very important messages.

One day Buddy didn't turn up for duty and Jeremy became very worried that he might not return. Another two weeks passed, but Buddy still hadn't returned.

Eventually one early morning in December 1979 while Jeremy was in bed but not asleep he heard a soft whispering voice called him, 'Jeremy!'

He sat up in bed to listen. He heard the voice again and turned his eyes around the room to find out where it had come from.

He saw Buddy outside the window looking through the glass trying to get his attention. Jeremy was glad to see Buddy and waved his hand, 'Hi, Buddy, Just a minute I'm coming.' He opened the window and the bird flew in quickly. He shut the window and sat on the side of his bed. 'Well, Buddy, what news have you brought at this time of the morning? And where have you been for the last two weeks?'

The sparrow ruffled up its feathers and looked at him with sad eyes. 'Are you ok, Buddy?' Jeremy asked.

'Yes,' the sparrow replied. 'I did go away but I heard a cry of desperation coming from a country in Europe where the missiles are hidden.' As soon as Buddy said this, Jeremy saw that Buddy was frightened about what was to come. 'Buddy, what was that cry you heard about?'

The sparrow shuffled once or twice and said, 'It is all about the six nuclear missiles which I told you about. They are lost from time and space so there is a danger they will accidentally explode.'

Jeremy thought that if the missiles went off some might be head towards Great Britain and others towards America.

This was a very frightening situation and he understood why the poor sparrow was so afraid. It could not face the danger alone. The bird knew perfectly well that it would be useless going alone to find the missiles.

'Jeremy,' the bird spoke, 'will you go with me to the place and help me search for the hidden missiles?'

As soon as the sparrow said this he and the bird found themselves in Europe where the bird said the missiles were hidden. Buddy said that the cry for help was coming from this area. Jeremy looked around the very remote place.

If there were an emergency it would be very unlikely if anyone would even know that they were there. Jeremy struggled through the rugged terrain which was many miles away from the nearest rural community.

Buddy flew past Jeremy saying, 'let me lead the search.'

'Ok,' Jeremy agreed.

They went on until they reached a certain location. Jeremy stood and watched attentively as the sparrow rested its tiny head on the ground to listen. 'Buddy, what on earth are you listening for?' Buddy turned its eyes sideways and looked at Jeremy. 'If the missiles are beneath the ground I will most likely hear them ticking.'

'Ticking,' Jeremy repeated frightened, whilst looking at the sparrow.

'Buddy,' Jeremy spoke, 'I can hardly believe this. Let's just say that we find the dangerous nuclear missiles. What are we going to do about them?'
    'Well,' the sparrow declared, 'if we come across them, all we have to do is not disturbing them. We will report them to the authorities. More than that, it's our spiritual abilities that have got us involved in this matter; we are here to help protect innocent people from danger. By doing so it might endanger our lives but we'll have to find the six missiles before they go off by accident.'

CHAPTER 30

THE COUNTDOWN

'Jeremy,' the sparrow said, 'the missiles have been buried for such a long time that might make them even more dangerous.'

Poor Jeremy was not only feeling anxious, but also extremely cold. Then the bird decided that they should extend the search deeper into the woodland. They went on searching even further away from the nearest village. The sparrow could see that Jeremy wasn't very happy.

If they could get to the nearest village he could talk with some of the local people without making them panic. Jeremy and Buddy were struggling on through the cold, thin air when suddenly and unexpectedly the ground began to shiver beneath them.

'Buddy, I think it's an earthquake.'

While Jeremy was looking for a safe place to shelter, five of the six nuclear missiles popped up from underground in creature form.

'Oh, my God,' Jeremy breathed out dumfounded. Buddy lifted up his wings to fly but couldn't.

Jeremy turned his frightened eyes and looked at the creatures. He could have panicked but tried to be brave.

Neither Jeremy nor Buddy expected to find the missiles in the form of creatures. Jeremy looked timidly towards heaven, 'Oh, Lord God our saviour, only you are able to save us from these ravenous beasts.' As soon as he prayed a sixth missile creature suddenly popped up from underground and camouflaged itself before Jeremy's eyes. The sixth missile creature was the deadliest of them all. The creature's two wings were of pure gold and its body was of shiny silver. The name, 'Unknown Creature' was written on its back like a logo printed on a piece of cloth.

Now that the creatures were camouflaged they couldn't be easily identified from each other. The transformation of the sixth creature had Jeremy dumfounded, as it began to talk in a human voice. It came to light that the creatures were representatives of a terrorist organisation. This was quite a parable for Jeremy to solve. The Unknown Creature had commissioned the others to fly and three of them planned to fly to Great Britain. The other three creatures were directed to fly to America. Now that Jeremy saw that the extremists were planning a secret attack on Britain and her allies he acted bravely.

He apprehended the sixth missile creature, which was the boss of the others.

'Unknown Creature, neither you nor any of your followers are allowed to leave this country'.

As soon as he said this, the Unknown Creature became angry. It turned its wide eyes to look at the others. They all began ticking as if they were about to detonate. Buddy knew quite well that should the creatures put their heads down to the ground and their bottoms towards the sky, hell's terror couldn't be more destructive.

The bird became scared and flew away. Jeremy began to run as fast as his legs could take him as he headed towards the village. While he was running the scene deepened and the vision that Jeremy was having vanished.

Next morning Jeremy woke up and reminded himself of the creatures that he had seen and the secret plan to attack innocent people. He thought of the tragedy if the creatures attacked, thousands of innocent people could die. His mind was in a complete jumble.

Jeremy thought that he should tell Detective Whoot about the sparrow story to put his mind at ease. He began thinking that the detectives might take action about the nuclear missiles and the creatures they had discovered who were planning a secret attack. Then the Government might tighten up the country's defences. There's an old saying that it is better to be safe than to be sorry and they could send a search party to Europe to discover the abandoned missiles.

But Jeremy didn't have any proof of the sparrow's revelations because it didn't leave a clue behind. He began thinking about the new millennium, which wasn't too far away. Perhaps the unknown creatures were warning the governments of the world that they should be more careful. The people of the nations were getting more and more violent and they had very little sympathy for the rest of humanity.

Then his thoughts went back to autumn 1983 and Jeremy and Sally were in bed. Sally was woken up early in the morning by the sound of something tapping on the bedroom window. She looked at Jeremy but he was fast asleep. She had forgotten that Jeremy had a friendly sparrow. Buddy had returned to visit Jeremy with some new revelations for him to write about, but that morning the sparrow had encountered another of the unknown creatures that had caused it to panic.

The bird had slept all through the night standing on a single strand of wire. Next morning the sparrow woke early and flew to a leafless tree searching for food, but didn't find a single worm. It flew off again and came to rest in the avenue where Jeremy lived and from where it started a new search. As it was searching it unexpectedly came upon another of the unknown creatures and was frightened out of its wits. At length, it regained its sanity and it came to rest on the window ledge of Jeremy's home. The bird was very afraid of the creature and looking for help it began pecking at the window. Sally woke up, but lay still in bed. She tried to ignore the noise but couldn't. The tapping was faint but constant. She became concerned, but her husband was asleep and she was very scared, not knowing what was out there. She lay still with her eyes open wide, hoping that the tapping would go away. Then to add to her fears, she saw a ghostly figure of something moving outside of the bedroom window. But the bedroom curtains were closed so it was difficult to see clearly what was behind the glass.

As the tapping continued her fear grew stronger so she decided to wake up her husband. 'Jeremy,' she shook him, 'wake up, I think there's something outside our window pecking at the glass.'

Instead of getting up Jeremy just lifted up his head and laid it down again on the pillows.

'I haven't heard a thing,' he said to his wife with a tired yawn. Buddy had been away so long he had forgotten about the bird.

He turned from one side to the other and went to sleep again.

'Oh, no,' she said fearfully. 'You're not going to sleep again.'

She shook him until he opened his eyes but he was still reluctant to get up out of bed. She thought that her husband was afraid and would rather not go and investigate. But it wasn't so and he had different thoughts. The house in which they lived was not far from the avenue and there was a telegraph pole near the corner of the wall. Bits of loose string might be dangling from the pole against the glass window that sounded like something tapping. Having all these thoughts he kept his head firmly on the pillow with his eyes open and his ears ready to listen.

Sally knew quite well that if her husband didn't go to the window to see what it was she'd have no rest so she kept nudging him.

When he had enough, he said, 'Sally my dear, you worry too much. I'll go and have a look if that will stop you worrying.'

So he got out of bed went towards the window on tiptoes.

Sally said, 'Darling, wait a minute!' and picked up a slipper. 'Take this with you. If anyone attacks you, let them have it.'

He caught the slipper and shook his head. 'Darling, you make me laugh!' The slipper was so flexible it wouldn't even hurt a fly! She immediately put on her dressing gown and with one slipper on her feet she went to the window and hid herself behind the long curtain. As soon as her husband made an attempt to open the window she held his hand back.

'Oh boy, can't we just call the police instead of opening the window? Just imagine, if something dangerous came in suddenly, what would we do then?'

Jeremy knew that she was scared but that wasn't going to stop him, so he gave the window a sudden tilt and it flew wide open. Then to their horror, something zoomed in so quickly they couldn't even recognise what it was.

'Wow!' He staggered back a little and his wife gave out an awful scream. The neighbours must have heard her panic and went to their windows to look outside.

It wasn't until she saw the little sparrow flying around the room that she breathed a sigh of relief. She slung herself down across her bed. 'Honestly,' she uttered, with one finger pointing at the sparrow. 'There are our burglars!'

Sally and her husband laughed almost to tears. By this time the sparrow came to rest on Jeremy's shoulder.

When Sally looked and saw the bird sat on her husband's shoulder she elegantly lifted herself up and sat on the side of her bed.

'Can I have it?' she pleaded.

Then she gently reached out her hand and took the sparrow from her husband's shoulder. She stroked it with one finger from its head down to its tail.

'It is beautiful,' she said. 'Can I keep it for a pet?'

Before Jeremy could reply she took the bird with her into the bathroom, took a towel and dried it off, as Buddy was a bit wet after being outside in the cold all night. Sally had a real surprise, as she didn't know that sparrow was able to talk. While she was making a fuss the bird ruffled its feathers and begun to talk in a human's voice.

The sparrow told Jeremy that while it was outside in the avenue seeking food it had suddenly come upon a very strange looking creature. It looked just like the sixth missile that they had seen before the creature formed, only much younger.

Its two wings were gold and its body was of shining silver!

'What!' Jeremy spoke with surprise.

He thought that another of the unknown creatures has been born in this country. He turned his head sharply and looked at the sparrow. 'Buddy, do you think it's the same unknown creature we saw before that now lives in this country?'

Sally looked at them but didn't know what to say. She was too astonished to talk and she had never heard of a talking sparrow before. She wasn't aware that her husband had a special gift that makes him one of the most extraordinary people.

Jeremy's life had been filled with mysteries and miracles and many revelations, which kept urging him to keep on writing. Jeremy put the sparrow on his shoulder and went outside into the avenue. To his great amazement there were thousands of angry birds making a noise. The neighbours' dogs were barking. People were coming out of their houses to see what was going on. The avenue was in absolute chaos.

As Jeremy was standing there another bird flew close to him and whispered in his ear, 'This is a political demonstration against the unknown creatures.'

Jeremy was speechless: he couldn't believe how quickly the word had spread. Many people had turned out to watch the birds demonstrating against the creatures.

Another of the birds said, 'The Unknown Creature, which the sparrow saw this morning was young by date but not by age.'

Jeremy thought of the parable – perhaps the unknown creatures have been here before. Then he further thought that the demonstrators might know that the unknown creatures are in the avenue hiding somewhere and would not stop protesting until they had left. One of the birds came to talk on behalf of the protesters. It said that nobody should go too near to the unknown creatures as they had deadly stings to which there was no antidote.

As soon as the bird said this, they all heard footsteps.

'The police are coming,' said one person and the crowd of birds went silent.

They all stood still and looked towards the lane to see who was coming. While they were all looking for the police, soldiers arrived instead. They came wearing their newly designed uniforms, made of a bright yellow plastic material.

As soon as the solders came into the view the protestors began shouting, 'Where are your guns?'

Instead of replying, one soldier took long vigorous strides and came into the midst of the protesters. He lifted up a hand and said, 'We haven't brought our guns because we're sure we can settle this matter without a fight.'

'Look at us,' one soldier said, let's have your attention.'

There all went quiet. 'We've brought you these yellow plastic uniforms. Please do not approach the unknown creatures unless you're wearing one of these.' Some of the protestors gave heed to the soldier's advice and some left the avenue confused.

The soldier shouted out again, 'Listen up, before you'll go. Have any of you seen the unknown creatures this morning?'

The crowd went silent each one looking at the other. The soldier knew then that none of them had actually seen the unknown creatures.

Then Buddy the sparrow flew from the branch of a tall leafless tree, which was at the corner of the avenue and came to rest on Jeremy's shoulder

'Ok, Buddy,' Jeremy said, 'you can come down from my shoulder. Tell the soldiers what you saw this morning.'

The soldiers were surprised as they had never heard a talking sparrow before, but they listened to what the bird had to say. As the day had grown much older, hundreds of protesters had left the scene and now just Jeremy, the soldiers and Buddy remained. The soldiers told Jeremy about a high security prison in Manchester, which they had made ready for the unknown creatures.

One soldier spoke of her disappointment that they had come so far but hadn't see the unknown creatures. As the soldiers were about to leave the avenue Jeremy took his notebook from his pocket and made a note of the yellow plastic material the soldiers were wearing to protect themselves from radiation. The soldiers had left their army truck at the top of the lane. As the soldiers and Jeremy were walking back the sparrow rested on Jeremy's shoulder. As soon as the soldier saw the sparrow he decided to take Jeremy and the bird to give evidence to the higher authorities. Before he drove away he picked up his army truck telephone and dialled a special code that connected him to an aerodrome, somewhere in Manchester and many miles away from where they were in Yorkshire.

The soldier gave his colleagues the bad news that they had not caught the unknown creatures but that they were still searching for them. Then he asked his colleagues, 'How is the new invention progressing?'

'Fine,' was the reply, 'soon our planes will be flying without any sound,' then the soldier in Leeds said to his colleague, 'You might not believe this, but I have a guy with me who has a talking sparrow. The sparrow saw the unknown creatures this morning. So, I'm taking them with me to the aerodrome in Manchester.'

When the soldier in Leeds had finished talking he said with a smile, 'That's great! That's great.'

He then took Jeremy and the talking sparrow with him and off they went to Manchester. As soon as they approached the M62 the new invention that the soldiers were talking about was already in progress. Instead of the old overhead traffic signals the police officers were on the motorway giving directions to the traffic. Some of them were fully armed with the modern weapons and dressed in their yellow plastic protective clothing. As the police officers suspected that the unknown creatures were subject to some type of radioactive disease they were also wearing the protective clothing. The soldier drove on and eventually they came to an interchange where many police officers were waiting. One officer stepped forward and lifted up his hand and the soldier slowed his vehicle to a stop.

The officer approached the driver, 'I have a message for you. It came from your army base. You should follow the motorway until you come to the first exit on the left hand side of the road and then drive until you come to a large common. Stop and wait there. Someone will escort you from there to the army lab.'

'Thank you officer,' said the soldier and drove on. After he had been travelling 30 miles he turned off the motorway. Soon he came to the common.

'This is it,' the soldier said. 'Jeremy, we'll wait here.'

So they waited at the common for about 20 minutes until they saw a jeep with two officers coming towards them.

The two officials got out of their jeep and the soldier saluted. 'Sir, I haven't caught the unknown creatures; they escaped before we got to the place this morning, but I've brought two witnesses who saw them.'

'Very well,' one officer said, 'we'll ask our two friends to make their statements here in the jeep.'

'Yes, sir,' agreed the soldier. Then he went and brought Jeremy and the sparrow to the jeep to meet the two army officers. The soldier was first to give his statement. Jeremy and the sparrow sat and listened. After the soldier had given his statement it was Jeremy and the sparrow's turn. The officers were very surprised to hear the sparrow give its statement in a human voice.

The creature had been on the run for a long time, but if it surrendered we could all live in peace. The officials finished taking their witness statements and were now ready to leave the common.

'Soldier,' one officer shouted.

'Sir,' replied the soldier with a salute.

'You can now take Jeremy and his talking sparrow back to their home in Yorkshire. Use one of our jeeps instead of the truck.'

The soldier acknowledged and the officials drove away. From the common it was about two miles drive until they came to an aerodrome and army barracks that was home to many soldiers. The soldier left Jeremy and his sparrow in the jeep and went to talk with his colleagues and returned with a reward for Jeremy and Buddy. He gave them £30 for finding the sixth creature with the deadly sting.

During the journey back to Leeds Jeremy took out his note-book and jotted down some of the things he had seen at the aerodrome. The most exciting was that the aeroplanes were taking off and landing without any noise! While they were driving on Dewsbury Road towards the city Jeremy looked out and saw one of his friends coming from a local coffee shop.

'Soldier,' Jeremy shouted, 'can you please let us get out here.'

Sure,' the soldier replied.

He looked in his mirror and lifted up his hand to say goodbye.

CHAPTER 31

THE SOLDIER'S LAB

As soon as Jeremy got out of the jeep Buddy flew away. 'Buddy,' he shouted, where are you going?' But the bird flew away without replying.

Then Jeremy saw one of his friends, Geoffrey Adamson who came across to meet him.

'Boy, I'm I glad to see you!' said Geoffrey. 'Where have you come from to be at this side of the city at this time of day? Just wait until you've heard what going on. You might not have heard this yet, but it seems that the city is going to be a ghost town at night fall.'

'What are you talking about? What's happened?' Jeremy asked, astonished.

Geoffrey looked at him with sadness in his eyes and pointed towards the police station. At the side of the road a large crowd of people was gathered outside the station. Jeremy thought that something terrible must have happened while he was in Manchester.

He and Geoffrey went towards the police station and soon found themselves in the middle of a large crowd of people. They were saying that the worst was to come at midnight.

Then suddenly and unexpectedly a large clock appeared in the thin air over the River Aire and a young lady at the police station began counting down to what she called the approaching hour of destruction, which was at midnight.

Jeremy could have panicked as he remembered the unknown creatures that were planning their escape from another country to Britain. Then the lady who was counting down stopped for a moment and a man made a public announcement over the microphone. He told the people that six missiles creatures had set off, but he didn't name the country. He said the missiles were heading towards Great Britain. When they heard this the crowd could have panicked.

CHAPTER 32

THE TALKING SPARROW

'Hello. Thank you for reading my story. I am Buddy the talking sparrow that you've been reading about. Well, I am still a close friend of Jeremy Ashman.

Now, can I tell you a little secret about me? Do you know that all of my friends, the other sparrows think I am a real bird? But they are so wrong.

I represent the spirit of Jeremy Ashman's visions and I came to him in sparrow form! That's why I'm able to talk but it is only those who have special abilities that can understand me! So I asked Jeremy to put my story in writing!

The fact remains that an ordinary sparrow does not talk. But I have an ability that enables me to see incoming danger and I would often tell Jeremy what I foresaw, so he could write about it and give out an early warning. We are still looking out for you. Please don't forget you're reading about me. Thank you very much. You can carry on reading now.'

By this time three of the missiles were on their way to America and two to Great Britain. The sixth missile creature was already somewhere in the country waiting for the others to arrive.

The army's spokesperson was at the University broadcasting the incoming danger. He said that the invasion was sudden and they had left it too late and the country was completely off its guard.

Jeremy took out his notebook and jotted down the date – 29 September 1990.

Geoffrey and Jeremy parted company. Jeremy went walking with some other people towards the city. When they arrived Jeremy was amazed at the crowd of people there.

He couldn't believe that there were so many brave people in Britain. Instead of the people leaving the city, which was threatened by a nuclear attack they were all there seeking immediate help from God.

If God did not send help quickly, by nightfall the city would be nothing more than a ghost town

A preacher was there preaching of the second coming of our Lord Jesus Christ. The crowd was huge, the preacher was fiery. Jeremy was just in time to hear the preacher say, 'Look up.'

They all turned their eyes and looked to the sky! The preacher said, 'Let this be known to all, it is written that men will cause judgement to come upon themselves.'

As soon as the preacher said this, he looked up and saw two deadly missiles appeared in the sky over the city. And he pointed to the sky, 'It is only God who is able to bring this world to its complete end.' Then he paused.

The crowd of people knelt down together and began to pray with eyes filled with tears. The Lord God of heavens must have heeded their prayers as, miraculously; the sun came out in the night with burning flames and burnt the missiles away in the sky! Not even the dust from them fell to the ground. All the people got up from their knees and gave thanks to the Lord, saying that He is our saviour indeed. All this was a call to remember the days and the times in which we live. After the great procession of prayer was over the scene deepened and the visions vanished away!

Jeremy woke suddenly from his sleep and was bewildered. He thought of the new millennium, which was near at hand, and how his vision might be leading up to the end of our time on earth.

Then he reminded himself of the first time he had seen the unknown creatures when they were calculating a time and a date on which they would put their secret plan into action. Could the new millennium be that time?

At the time of his vision he was standing among a crowd of people and suddenly a large clock had appeared above the River Aire and begun ticking down towards the approaching time of the incoming destruction.

However, that scene had vanished and a few months had passed. Jeremy took a day off, leaving Detective Sergeant Keen to work with Detective Doctor Whoot until his return. Now he was free to spend a little time with his wife and family.

ABOUT THE AUTHOR

Ivan Golding was born in the Parish of Manchester Jamaica, West Indies. He came to England to live in the early sixties. Since then he and his family had many of ups and downs in their lives. But they lived in hope of better and prosperous Britain full of God loving people.